NOT INDIAN ENOUGH

NOT INDIAN ENOUGH

SUMATI HUBER

NU VOICE PRESS

First published by NU VOICE PRESS 2024
An imprint of Hubhawks Pvt. Ltd
www.nuvoicepress.com

This is a work of fiction. Space and time have been rearranged to suit the convenience of the book. Except for public figures, hotels, and institution names, any resemblance to persons living or dead or the real events are purely coincidental. The opinions expressed in the book are those of the characters, and should not be confused with that of the Author.

ISBN: 978-81-970218-1-7

Typeset by Saanvi Graphics, Noida

Printed at Manipal Technologies Limited, Manipal

Published by Nu Voice Press

To my dear husband Franz, the most Indian non-Indian person I have ever met, who has strangely helped me become more Indian. My rebellion may have peaked when we started dating but our story is just starting now with our wonderful children.

To my son Riyan and daughter Amani, may you both grow up to be strong and independent like your mom and always stay true to your voice. But don't even think about acting the way I did growing up or I will send you both to a boarding school in a remote village in India. Besides, I hope this book doesn't embarrass you when you're old enough to read it.

And to my parents without whom I would never have had boundaries to rebel against. Thank you for trying to keep me in check but also allowing me to find my own path because you didn't know what it actually meant to ground me.

What Kind of Rebel Are You?

Seriously, no one in this family understands me. I'd rather stay locked up in my room than go out there and listen to them tell me I'm wrong about everything, yet again. At least I have my computer in here to keep me company. I wonder if there are any searches for "Why are Indian parents so crazy?" or "How can I be myself when no one gets me?" Let me check.

Oh, what's this quiz? "What kind of rebel are you?"

I definitely need to take it...

There's more to being Indian than attending or planning weddings or being asked when your marriage will take place. In fact, there are many nuances to your behavior that determine whether you're the sort of delightful catch that aunties will brag about to their sons, or you'll be *that girl* stumbling out of the *sangeet* with your sari unraveling and shoes missing (*true story*).

Take this totally unscientific quiz to find out where you fall on the scale from respectable to rebellious.

1. **You're an unmarried girl at a wedding and every auntie is asking, "When's your turn?" What most sounds like your reply?**

A) "Oh, I've already been married twice! I guess I totally forgot to invite you to both of my weddings! This is awkward…"

B) "Thank you for asking. I haven't found anyone yet."

C) "I've visited over 50 pundits and astrologers and given them the date, time and place of my birth. Looks like the stars are not aligning with me just yet. What woe has befallen me? I'm sure after I channel my good Hindu side and perform acts of worship with several pujas, it will all be OK and I'll find my perfect karmic match."

2. **Complete the sentence: Miniskirts are…**

A) The best thing since sliced bread. That's obviously why they sliced the skirt too.

B) Appropriate at the beach — but only when you're on a trip with friends, not family.

C) Best used as a dishcloth.

3. **In history class, when Mr. Patel brought up the "British Raj", what was your response?**

A) "How do you know my cousin Raj in Manchester?"

B) "I know it was the time of British rule in India, but I need to ask Professor Google for more details."

C) "Well, *<adjusts monocle, tightens suspenders>* history books state that the British Crown established its control in the Indian subcontinent from 1858 to 1947 and the numerous events that took place during this time are extremely important in understanding modern-day India."

4. What's your biggest fashion regret?

A) Not having a pierced belly button/tramp stamp to flaunt with your crop top.

B) Wearing the wrong underwear resulting in visible panty lines.

C) Showing too much ankle.

5. Solve this puzzle: Sonia is married to Sanjay, who has three brothers named Kunal, Sunil and Anoop. They are married to Dimple, Poonam and Sangeeta, respectively. Every evening, Kunal and Sunil meet up with their second cousins twice removed from their father's side to have some masala chai and talk about business. With this information, please figure out how many spoons of sugar Sanjay takes with his tea.

A) WTF?!

B) It depends on how many biscuits he consumes with his tea.

C) Two-and-a-half.

6. What would your shaadi.com matrimonial ad sound like?

A) What's shaadi.com?

B) All castes accepted. All credit cards accepted too.

C) Homely girl with fair-to-wheatish complexion seeks lifelong mate of good family, character and profession.

7. Describe your ideal first date outfit.

A) That skintight little black dress that leaves little to the imagination.

B) The safe high-low dress you reserve for important events.

C) A bridal *lehenga* because you plan to meet your date for the first time at your wedding. (A lehenga is a long, beautiful skirt worn by women in South Asia that is often elaborately embroidered but you already knew that unless you're not Indian enough.)

8. What would gossip about you sound like?

A) She dresses slutty, she drinks too much, she has been known to fraternize with multiple men.

B) She needs subtitles to understand Bollywood movies.

C) That one time she under-fried the samosas before serving them.

9. You're about to leave the house and your parents demand you go back to your room and change. (Yes, you still live at home with your family.) What do you do?

A) Scream, "Ugh! You guys totally don't understand *fah-shawn*!", then go on a tirade about how you saw Auntie Roly's daughter wearing something way worse and much shorter last week before you storm out of the house in a huff… then come home way past curfew.

B) Change the offending article of clothing but keep everything else intact.

C) This has never happened to me.

10. In three words you are…

A) Unconventional, daring, creative.

B) Pleasant, respectful, nonchalant.

C) Seeking, a, husband.

IF YOU ANSWERED…

MOSTLY A's: Welcome Rebel! Before you read any further, please take a moment and apologize to your parents for all those sleepless nights and stress you have caused them. Oh! Forgive me, rebels don't apologize. After all, why should you say sorry when you feel like you're the only person who understands you? Although you may spend more time defending your individualistic choices — friends, relationships, that "not wearing pants" is a real fashion statement — you actually love the fact that while everyone else is taking part in choreographed wedding dances, you get to hang out at the bar and flirt with boys.

MOSTLY B's: Hi there, lovely! Yes, I realize one of you reading this may be named "Lovely" given the trend of Indian nicknames. But nonetheless, you are generally considered quite a doll for your affable nature. You're not out to shake up society or defy anyone per se, but you do sometimes find yourself wondering why it's acceptable to expose so much skin in a sari, but not in a bikini. Your general idea of rebelling is taking a photo in front of a "No Photo" sign… but we love you anyway.

MOSTLY C's: *Namaste* to the dream daughter! Your parents must have done something right in their last life to be blessed with a child like you. Obedient, agreeable and respectful, you listen to your elders and study hard in school. The first time your mom asked you to learn how to cook, you happily went into the kitchen, instead of saying you were too busy scrolling on your phone. Now, your roti is rounder and fluffier than anyone else's in the house. Even though some of us may be acting out currently and thinking we know better, you're the one we'll eventually seek advice from when we don't know what to do with our own rebellious daughters.

Wow! I answered "A" for every question. At least there's someone out there who can relate to what I go through. I can't be alone in my struggle.

I am Sanjana, Indian by name and confused everywhere else.

This is my story.

CHAPTER 1

When Clothes and Culture Clash

"Don't even think about leaving the house in that disgusting underwear!" my mom yelled as I tried to nonchalantly brush past her.

Damn!

I HAD been hiding in my bedroom with my ear against the door, beads of nervous sweat adding a water mustache to my already hairy upper lip as I waited for a safe moment to emerge. The sounds of my mom furiously washing and clanking utensils at the kitchen sink located just outside my room made my heartbeat jump outside my body. She loved to turn herself into the most infuriating human alarm clock to prevent her lazy daughter from sleeping in, especially on early Saturday mornings. When the torrential water stream stopped running and my mom's footsteps became more distant, I presumed the coast was clear.

It was time to execute my stealth exit. I mentally mapped out my Indian family obstacle course — a blueprint one must memorize if you have any hope of leaving unscathed from a joint household. I quietly cracked open the door and confirmed the kitchen was empty. I took a few cautious steps out and stopped before approaching the living room just around the corner. The Lazy Boy was halfway reclined with my dad occupying his seat in front of the TV. A golf tournament was playing on the screen in the background at a low volume which certainly meant my dad was dozing off and wouldn't notice me. *This is what it must feel like to be lentils in a pressure cooker,* I thought to myself as I dashed past my drowsy dad.

I tiptoed towards the next hurdle — my grandparents' room. *Dadi*, my paternal grandmother, spent most of her time occupied with her Zee TV programs. Hindi voices would keep blasting from beyond the door she always kept slightly ajar, so she could easily shout out whenever she needed something. If her show was particularly scandalous, I would have to endure a painful lecture on how I dress up like the "girls of today". Those girls who feature on her TV serials had no clue how to tie up their hair into a nice bun or make round rotis. Phew, I managed to dodge that for today and avoided a 15-minute delay. My water mustache started to evaporate and I could finally start breathing normally again.

All I had left to do was make it out the front door. All that stood between me and my freedom was ten small steps. I was just about to make it when I heard her.

"Don't even think about leaving the house in that disgusting underwear!" my mom yelled as I tried to nonchalantly brush past her.

Damn!

"But mom it's not even that bad!" I pleaded. "Please!"

"You think Auntie Dimple's daughter, Rimple walks around like that?" she sneered. "Go change your clothes now! It's bad enough you don't know how to do anything at all. Now, you want to go out with your friends dressed like that? What will dadi say if she sees you?"

"But mom, I've seen Auntie Dimple's daughter Rimple wear much worse! And Rimple is always talking to boys! You don't even know! You only know what Auntie Dimple tells you!"

It was a lost cause. I begrudgingly trudged back to my room, stopping to look at my sad reflection in the hallway mirror. *Great job, Sanjana. You can't even succeed in leaving the house without getting scolded.*

I am twelve years old with a mustache that rivals pubescent boys of my own age. My frizzy black hair is always pulled back in a ponytail, to show off my chubby face and hairy sideburns that extend all the way under my chin. I am wearing a striped V-neck t-shirt that makes me look more horizontal than I already am. But that isn't the problem. The problem is my denim shorts.

Secretly rebelling under the pile of good girl pants in my closet are two pairs of shorts. I had bought them under the influence of my friends who convinced me I looked really cool in them. "But what will my mom say?" I remember asking. They looked confused in response, which should have been my first obvious sign to avoid putting controversial shopping decisions in the hands of my non-Indian pals.

While my friends wore cutoffs with reckless abandon and never had to worry about attending mandatory family dinners, going to the temple or hiding their boyfriends, all my choices — sartorial or otherwise — were scrutinized through the conservative lens of my Indian clan. Donning shorts was enough to be branded as scandalous; the mere sight of exposing your legs would somehow allow hungry boys to sniff you out and ruin all your chances of getting married into a "good family". Or so my parents believed.

Trying to rectify what it means to be an Indian girl living in a globalized world can be frustrating. Born in Bangkok and raised by American TV, I struggled to find the balance between respecting old-fashioned traditions and the allure of the "I can do whatever I want when I turn 18", mentality.

My family carried fears from their worldview that didn't match the world I lived in — when a girl reaches a certain age and her hormones kick in, showing too much skin can be considered unsafe. It may attract unwanted attention and temptation from men who haven't been taught how to respect women or control their inhibitions. Pronounced gender roles come into play here with the way a woman presents herself. Clothes speak to our privilege, class, status and education. "People will think we don't have enough money to afford the rest of the material that should cover your legs," my dad would quip whenever I pointed out that many other girls wear shorts.

Another harsh truth I noticed is that the negative attention and tsk-tsk-ing predominantly come from nosy gossipmongers in our own society and even from our trusted circle of people — those we invite to tea parties, dinners and weddings. These individuals, affectionately termed as "aunties" possess an unmatched ability to judge a girl and make rude assumptions about her character based on their definition of "provocative" dressing. Their opinions trickle back to our parents who would rather eliminate the feeling of shame than tell these aunties to mind their own business.

My twelve-year-old self could sense the hypocrisy of being vilified by the same aunties. These were the ones who freely exposed their roti-filled bellies in saris but were ready to tear down girls who showed skin through other attire. Isn't it more important to change this behavior than to make a girl feel bad for her wardrobe choices?

That's how the rebel in me was born.

That first pair of shorts I wore not only exposed the ingrown hairs on my legs but also my mind to the double standards that women face. I began to see how females were branded based on how they chose to attire themselves.

My whole adolescence consisted of being sent back to my room to change items of clothing or alter my outfits. These battles often ended up with me immaturely yelling, "I can't wait till I move out so I can wear whatever I want!"

The funny thing is that since I've moved out, I now check all the important boxes that determine if you're a well-rounded and "complete" Indian woman. If this had taken place in any other order than what is listed, my story may have ended more dismally:

✓ *I found a suitable man.*

✓ *I got married to him.*

✓ *I've had babies with him.*

And yet I'm still afraid to wear shorts in front of my parents!

It seems no matter how old I get and my life roles change from a snarky teenager to an outgoing college student to now nagging wife and overprotective mother, I'm still silently burdened by societal and cultural restrictions.

Fashion is a loud and powerful tool to combat the restrictions wisely. Style is a way for me to tell a different story every day and express my true self. Any fear of judgement is tossed out like last season's shoes. My closet is my strongest weapon.

Now, if only I can find something to wear.

CHAPTER 2

Two-Timing Traits

TRADING the possibility of Tata cars for *tuk-tuks*, my paternal grandfather left the great state of Punjab in 1938 to travel to Thailand. The weeks-long journey began on a ship from Kolkata to Penang, Malaysia, where he then boarded a train that took him to Bangkok. A textile shop started by his elder brother in 1923 was waiting for him. He was 16, fresh out of high school and ready to join the family business. Many families from the same and nearby villages in Punjab had also migrated to Thailand because you know we Indians like to travel in large packs.

Thailand offered the opportunity for enterprising Indians to establish new businesses. They had served as mainly landlords in India competing with other family members, and came abroad seeking alternative economic ventures. India is known for its large textile industry and they brought the knowledge of this trade with them to Thailand. It is likely that a few families found financial success working with fabrics in Thailand

and once the news traveled, others followed suit. No word if aunties also helped spread the word by sharing every detail and gossiping while they were all getting their hair blow-dried at the same salon.

With some arranged marriages and active matchmaking from the original elders, the Indian community in Bangkok began to flourish. Our close-knit Punjabi network consisted of families with similar experiences as mine. We all had grandparents who had migrated to Thailand as first-generation Indian immigrants and planted the seeds for our lives to grow here.

They opened their businesses in the same area within Bangkok's Chinatown, pretty much identical fabric shops next door to each other, just with different family names on the company plaque outside. Their children and grandchildren, such as myself, were all born here with each generation assimilating more to Thailand's lifestyle and habits than the ones before.

I came into the world making a fiercely dramatic entrance that would foreshadow my existence into a society that I would spend much of my life rebelliously navigating. One look at me emerging with my full head of black hair, and you could say that I was undeniably Indian, but bestowed with a Thai passport to further muddle my character. Growing up in a foreign country that my family had adopted as our home meant that our predecessors had to work extra hard to ensure that we retained our Indian identity, a common scenario experienced by many who leave their native land for new frontiers. The first wave of Indians who had come to Thailand steadfastly tried to maintain their traditions from the motherland. This was no easy feat as the world is large, yet connected all at once and we were readily exposed to the temptations of other cultures that are seemingly more "liberating". My grandfather's father was one of the few who left Thailand to return to Punjab. There were too many non-vegetarian food options here and the openness of the culture didn't bode well with him.

My parents, although both born in Bangkok, still stood by their responsibility to force me to abide by what they thought was the proper code of conduct for an Indian girl. They encouraged me to seek out like-minded friends (translation: brown people).

Learning Hindi was non-negotiable and Sunday mornings were spent with a teacher who probably wished she had chosen a different profession than having to deal with a pupil like me. I would rather hide in the bathroom for the whole hour than perfect the nasal sounds of the alphabet.

From a young age I was put on display in horrible, frilly outfits on stage to perform badly-choreographed dances at weddings of relatives I didn't know. Later, women in saris would painfully pinch my cheeks and rotate 100-baht banknotes clockwise over my head. This ritual symbolizes bestowing of blessings and removal of negative energy, which was probably necessary after the audience members had to suffer through my performance.

Training to be a "good Indian girl" also involved being sent to Hindu religion classes to recite prayers that I still don't comprehend, much to the chagrin of the many Gods, I'm sure. Once, my super-religious mom was mortified when I forgot my manners and extended my left hand to receive *prasad*, a religious offering that has been blessed by a pundit and given to devotees at the end of a puja. "Right hand!" she shrieked under her breath while swatting the offending limb away.

To Indians the left hand is meant for cleansing and washing oneself, thus it is considered unceremonious to offer up this unwanted palm for acts involving religious rites, eating, cooking and handing over money — another fun fact of my culture that was lost on me.

It wasn't my parents' fault that their rebellious daughter couldn't be molded into the Indian girl that they hoped.

It was difficult for me to identify with my Indian-ness because I didn't understand it. It was like everyone else was reading from the same book but my copy somehow had the pages ripped out that would have illuminated the answers. Everything I was told to do seemed superficial without explanation or reason. I had an Indian name and Indian appearance, but these were not factors in my control. We just had to accept the way things were. Trying to question or revolt against it caused a chain reaction of dismay from our family and the larger community.

Here I was in a country that was dominated by Thai people, food and customs. We had already shed our Indian surnames for long, unpronounceable Thai ones on all our official documents. How was I supposed to immerse myself and adopt the traditions of a land I no longer belonged to, a land I only visited occasionally during summer vacation after I had been approved with a tourist visa?

When would I speak Hindi if I didn't live in India? Why was I being forced to eat watery *saag paneer* (cottage cheese cooked with spinach and Indian spices) when *pad kra pao gai* (stir-fried Thai basil chicken) was more readily available? (How do you even buy saag from the supermarket without knowing what it's called in Thai?) What was the point of wearing Indian clothes if everyone else was wearing Western clothes? Even the most patient of parents cannot answer their annoying child's inquiries about every decision they make, so my cultural education never quite took off. The Indian parents' handbook for raising children didn't include an extensive chapter on what to do when bombarded with questions. *"That's just how we do things"*, *"As long as you live under my roof, you need to do as you are told"*, *"My house, my rules"*, were the repetitive responses that stopped any constructive discussions and compromises from taking place.

Despite any limitations I faced socially or sartorially, one aspect my parents evolved on was education regardless of gender. My brothers and I were afforded this equally, regardless of other patriarchal problems that were unconsciously ingrained in our upbringing. Even if we made any other mistakes in life, they would never allow any meddling society-auntie/uncle to say we were anything but smart, studious and stellar in school.

My mother, a straight A+ student, loved homework. If our teachers didn't give us school-work, she would create her own for us. She believed everything was made better with perfect handwriting and spent hours poring over our penmanship in assignments.

"What is that, a bindi?" she retorted whenever I was feeling creative and drew my full stops a bit too large, resembling the dot worn at the center of the forehead by Indians. She made me erase it and do it again, pointedly and precisely. Despite it being cute and trendy, dotting i's with hearts was frivolous to her and wouldn't win any points in furthering our education.

My mom secretly enjoyed playing "teacher" to us because it was her dream career that she was unable to pursue. My mother had attended a prestigious private high school which was the norm for families who could afford it. Despite their economic standing, her parents didn't believe it was necessary or safe for her to continue with a university education. She was told her future would involve staying home and performing traditional housewife duties, the same roles she had seen all the women in her life play.

My mom, a rebel in her own right, fought incessantly with her parents for a chance to go to college and shockingly, *abroad.* Dreams of studying in London remained dreams. She often lamented that in her generation it wasn't common for women to have jobs, so her parents didn't invest in further studies beyond high school. She settled for enrolling in a local secretarial program that taught skills such as shorthand, typing and basic marketing. She soon got married at 23 and her life quickly became what they said it would be — usurped by her obligations to her family and three children.

My parents enrolled all their children in a private international school in Bangkok based on the American education system. There were limited options for local Indian schools and Thai public schools weren't known for fostering critical thinking. This is where I would spend my whole childhood from first grade until high school graduation.

Going to an academic institution is a privilege but being immersed in an international environment would lead to even more struggles about our identity and upbringing.

Suddenly, I was exposed to kids from all types of backgrounds, and more so, tempted by how they seemed more unburdened than the conservative shackles I was bound by.

There were girls who came to school with their hair down! They had never heard of the benefits of ghee! They weren't made to sleep with their hair in a braid! Their moms didn't lather them in coconut oil! They wore short skirts! Their legs and arms were naturally hairless!

They were Thai, Indian, Singaporean, American, German, Cambodian, Swedish, Icelandic, Australian — you see it on a map, and they were there! A smorgasbord of nationalities in one place. Our school tried to celebrate our unique ethnicities with annual international day parades where we showed off food and dress from our various cultures. I proudly brought samosas, the most basic item that even non-Indians can identify and wore an itchy *salwar kameez,* even though I was already harboring my first dark secret about being Indian.

My accent.

At home, my family and I spoke English. We all had a distinct Indian undertone to our speech which was conditioned in me from being around numerous relatives in my formative years. However, at school I realized no one sounded like me. In fact, almost everyone — including the teachers — had an American accent. Even the accent of other Indians sounded westernized!

Maybe I was embarrassed to sound Indian, or I thought I was supposed to speak a certain way at school. Thick Indian accents had historically been parodied and mocked, and I certainly wasn't going to be the girl that got made fun of. Even at seven years old, I sensed I would fit in better if I adopted an American accent to use with anyone who was non-Indian.

I don't know if I would call it "fake" because after a while, it became second nature to me and this learned parlance would automatically come out depending on who I was speaking to.

It was problematic though when I was in the same room with both my Indian family and non-Indian friends and I had to switch between accents. I would be worried my two-timing tongue would be found out. But even to this day, I can never speak in my Indian accent to any non-Indian person no matter how much I try to force it out.

I always felt conflicted due to this trait because I ended up asking myself, which tone is the "real" me? Would boyfriends truly know me if I couldn't speak to them in my mother accent (this is because I obviously assumed they would be non-Indian)? Could I have given better presentations at school if I spoke as a smarter sounding Indian? Did my family think I was ashamed of my heritage by trying to quash it with my speech?

This clash of identities extended itself into my dress. Like the two different accents I could switch on and off depending on the company I was in, I could apply the same formula to my clothing choices. I figured out early on — nuanced ways of dressing up — depending on whether I was with my conservative clan or the cool friends I had made at my international school.

I am ten years old and my family and I are preparing to go to the airport for a short weekend getaway to Singapore. My aunt joins us on this trip. She is in our living room sipping tea while we wait for the suitcases to be loaded into the car. When it is time to leave, I grab my prized Skechers. They are blue and gray and have no laces, a total fashion win for the 90s. I pull down my socks so that they would hide under the shoes (no-show socks aren't prevalent yet) and make two equal folds up on my pant legs, an early "jean cuffing" statement before it was called as such.

(The Skechers brand wasn't sold in Thailand during those years, so it was even more of a status symbol if you had a pair. It meant you or someone you knew could afford to go to America to buy it.)

I am ready to roll with my exposed ankles that help draw more attention to my coveted slip-on sneakers.

"Sanjana, what are you doing? That's not how we wear pants." My normally friendly and supportive aunt zaps me with those words. I am taken aback.

It feels like a drive-by style shooting.

I try to tell her that this was how I always styled those jeans because the bottoms flare out quite a bit and go over my shoes. But while I stumble on my explanation, she tells me to pull down the folds and "cover my ankles". Is she really trying to protect me from getting mosquito bites on my leg? Does she want me to not feel cold on the airplane? Or is this the covered-up reality Indian girls face?

My individuality was being ripped from me. I had no freedom to dress how I wanted. It was just a tiny bit of ankle and who the hell was it hurting? These naysayers didn't understand that there were other ways to wear jeans than in its full length, expected form.

What would they say about wearing an oversized men's shirt as a dress? Sweatpants with heels as formal wear? A skirt as a tube top? All the creativity I had envisioned to getting full use of my clothing suddenly vanished. I started second-guessing all my style ideas. Why would I even bother trying to dress in a cool and distinct manner if no one could understand why I cuffed my jeans?

I acquiesced to my aunt's request to pull down my ankle folds. But I sulked the whole way to the airport, on the flight and perhaps am still sulking a little bit about it today.

CHAPTER 3

Daddy's Covered Up Girl

I HAD a wonderful and chubby childhood, but felt the pinch of being the only girl in a family dominated by boys. With two brothers and at least fifteen male first cousins, it was no secret to me that Indian families traditionally revere sons. They are the great brown hope for mothers. Historically, Indian sons are expected to live with their parents even after they get married, to take care of them financially and emotionally. Sons continue the family lineage and uphold its institutions. Age-old Hindu customs task sons with the significant responsibility of performing the last rites of their parents by lighting the funeral pyre, an act that is believed to provide eternal nirvana by breaking the cycle of rebirths.

Girls? Well, they can be perceived as a burden, in constant need of protection and defended from — you guessed it — the same boys that are worshipped. Girls "marry out" of their birth family and become absorbed in their duties to their husband and new parents. Not to mention, the bride's families are traditionally expected to provide a dowry to the groom, whether through money or property, making them a potential expensive investment with little return.

So, it's no surprise that my lack of Y chromosome following my elder brother's arrival wasn't met with the same jubilation. I was often told the story of how my father, who was overseas on a business trip at the time of my birth, received a somber phone call informing him, almost apologetically, that he now had a daughter. "The nurses say she is the loudest one in the nursery of the babies born today. We named her Sanjana," my grandfather told him over the phone. "It means 'gentle' just like daughters should be."

From early on my set of rules and expectations were extremely different from my brothers. If I didn't know better, I would have stayed silent, but everything around me opened up a whole world of progressive ideals. That lent itself to many tantrums and the first seeds of rebellion were taking root. There were disparities on where we were allowed to go, who we could hang out with, the chores we were required to complete (translation: the chores were mostly for me, the boys had none). My family didn't intentionally set out to be unfair. These were the gender roles that they had grown up with and didn't know any other way to treat a girl other than what had been instilled in them. From their point of view, they believed this was how I would be well-bred and successful in the future, but more importantly shape me into someone they could understand and identify with. I became none of those things.

It is tough to raise a good Indian girl, let alone bring them up overseas, as parents have to be more rigid in keeping their customs alive in their surrogate home. Sometimes new traditions and festivals emerge that aren't even celebrated in India, and beliefs may sometimes be more stringent as a way to preserve a sense of shared identity.

In Bangkok it was common for parents to throw a lavish first Diwali celebration for their son, with many families following the fading ritual of creating a *hatti* (a model replica of the ambitions parents have for their boy's future). The hatti would be showcased front and center at the event which displayed elaborate 3D miniature models of things like buildings to represent dreams of their son becoming a businessman, or a train set to indicate he could be an engineer. Did the same occur for a daughter's first Diwali celebration? Not mine at least.

Perhaps my father felt sorry that the culture I belonged to was accustomed to treating girls unfairly, but he didn't actually know how to overhaul the whole system. He took me under his wing and doted lots of attention on me. From childhood throughout my teens, my mom and I constantly battled. She perceived me as lazy for loving to sleep, found my desire to go out with friends unproductive and thought my interest in makeup and clothes would serve no purpose in life. "What did I do in my past life to have such a daughter?" she moaned, echoing the sad sentiment she must have heard during her own childhood and all the generations that came before her.

My dad tried to alleviate some of these conflicts by trying to bond with me through shopping. Almost every Sunday evening, he would take me to the mall, just the two of us, and actually enjoy the process of helping me pick out clothes. Those moments helped me feel some semblance of individuality, but only as much as could be rationed to an Indian girl. As the world evolves day by day, changing even the best held mindsets is like trying to pull off a pair of sticky leather pants in extreme humidity.

At the department store, my dad would walk around the women's clothing section first, while he touched and examined the fabrics used. My family had continued the textile business after my grandfather, so he was actually looking to see if any cloth had come from our factory.

Every time he said, "This is our fabric," I would also reach out to feel the cloth, feeling such pride that our family's special polyester blend had been used to create garments that manufacturers wanted ladies to wear. My dad had to know what colors and prints were in each season and could educate me on the history of jacquard or differentiating maroon versus burgundy.

Dads are actually the best people to trust for honest fashion advice. They won't censor their opinion if something looks weird on you. As a dad, he's not that concerned about protecting your ego and can easily veto any item that he deems inappropriate.

My father believed I could do anything "within reason" but of course that changed according to the circumstance.

He took notice of the environment I was being raised in, and tried to be comparatively liberal and balanced when it came to raising a daughter. He occasionally agreed to let me meet my friends at night, often against the wishes of my mom and grandparents. They told him it looked bad to let a girl go out alone. Of course, they didn't feel the same way when my brothers went out.

Dad did call me a million times when I was out of his sight but that's the price you pay for a bit of Indian girl freedom. "Sanjana" showed up row after row on his recently-called list on his phone and I was the first name added to his "Favorites" screen, even above his wife. Not because I was his favorite but because I was needed to be tracked most often. The incessant calling got to the point where I renamed his contact in my phone as "DANGER! DANGER!" to remind myself it was time to come home when I saw that flash on the screen.

The other catch was that he had his own specific ideas of how a girl should present herself and he had no qualms about imparting them to me.

Through my dad I learned important and lifelong fashion lessons. These included — high heels are "dangerous ladders", my purple smokey eye makeup was reminiscent of "a Halloween night where I received two black eyes" and oversized sunglasses made me look like a "bumblebee who got lost on the way to an audition for a Bollywood film".

Oh, and that no way in hell was he going to allow his daughter to wear sleeveless clothing.

The first and only time I ever used a curse word at my father was over a shirt he wouldn't let me buy.

I am eight years old.

We are at the department store and I am painfully attached to a frayed tie-dye tank top. I had seen something similar in one of my American teen fashion magazines where the bubbly blonde model wore it with white shorts and classic white Keds. It was effortless but so powerful. I needed to be that girl.

The rules of propriety as I interpreted it meant I was too scared to wear anything besides long-sleeved boring stripes and way-below-the-knee flowery dresses for fear of my family's disapproval. Now, I finally found the piece that would harness the cool style I had hidden within me. My friends were going to bow down to my edgy fashion sense.

My dad refused to buy the shirt. "It's torn and looks cheap," he said, although it surprisingly was quite expensive considering its tattered state. I begged, I pleaded. I wanted to escape the visions of a life full of basic fashion purgatory where I would forever be confined to monotonous stripes and safe flowery dresses. How could I ever truly style myself with the conservative viewpoints I was imprisoned by?

"No. I'm not going to buy it. We don't wear torn clothing. It doesn't even cover your arms."

"I said no."

"It's not even nice. No, stop making a scene. Control yourself. We are leaving now."

Then it came out…

"Asshole."

The look on my dad's face is one that is permanently etched in the part of my brain that stores the many terrible things I have done over the years.

It was a look of shock that was quickly replaced by sadness followed by anger.

My dad walked away.

Knowing I had done something irreversibly unspeakable, I quickly followed behind him out of the store. His head stayed fixed forward as he went straight towards the escalator. Assuming he was going to use it, I stepped on the first moving step. When I was halfway up, I turned around to see that my dad had tricked me! He had left me to go on the escalator by myself while he stayed downstairs.

Well-played, dad.

Nevertheless, considering I was only eight, he must have seen the fearful look on my face, a memory that is now permanently etched in the part of his brain where he stores his parenting regrets over the years.

I never did get that shirt and my dad eventually rescued me from the top of the escalator where I was standing stunned. This incident was pivotal in teaching me that my family's conservative viewpoints would be an issue in preventing me from dressing and acting the way I wanted to, and also make *me* behave like the real asshole.

My sneaky self had to find savvy ways to leave the house in clothes I knew my parents would never approve of.

That's how I came to rely on the trusty, if not impractical, cardigan trick.

Sleeveless attire can be frowned upon for nice Indian girls, although I was not convinced why anyone would have been swayed by my hairy and flabby arms. I mean, they were just limbs, right? A bunch of bones covered in skin. Who decided it was too provocative to show off bare shoulders and ashy elbows in Indian culture and attract unwanted attention? Is that why it's preferred for women to use their arms for things like child rearing, cooking and housekeeping?

All I knew was that I lived in a sweltering tropical country, and my sweat glands and I agreed that wearing as little clothing as possible was necessary for survival. The conservative powers that be didn't share my sentiment and insisted that I keep everything hidden from prying public eyes.

That didn't stop me when it came to meeting my group of friends outside. Everyone knows that girls have to dress alike lest they be branded as the less popular one of the group, or so we are fooled into believing when we are young and impressionable.

My friends would show up at the mall wearing spaghetti straps paired with short-shorts; cropped tube tops paired with cool baggy jeans; halter tops and floral miniskirts. Basically, every article of clothing that my dad would forbid me from buying in his presence. So, I had to slyly procure them when he was not around.

The only way to leave the house was to cover up the offending garment until I was a safe distance away. Later, I could strip off the unnecessary layers to show my true fashion self.

I didn't own many sweaters due to the climate of Bangkok. Our seasons are hot, hotter and hottest, so long sleeves only resulted in unsightly armpit stains and that is yet to be the latest trend to walk down the runway at fashion week.

I had two cardigans to choose from: a stained off-white one and a baggy periwinkle blue one that looked like it came from my grandma's closet. Neither was very attractive, and I certainly wouldn't choose to incorporate them into any outfit, except to hide what I was really wearing underneath.

When my inappropriate sleeveless base attire was complete, I threw on whichever one of these two cardigans I spotted first. It looked completely out of place. Bits of fringe, lace, satin or sequin would be peeking out from underneath the sweater; but I was OK suffering through a short-term fashion mishap until I could actually reveal my true outfit.

The other problem with this method was that I had to lug around a purse big enough to stash the sweater when I was ready to disrobe, hindering my ability to accessorize to my fullest potential. It required lots of trickery and adjustments just to be able to wear a sleeveless blouse. The reward was triumphing in my own style, the penalty was becoming a girl that you needed to keep an eye on. I'm 100% sure my parents knew exactly what I was doing, even though I was naive enough to think I could outsmart them.

As soon as I approached the mall or wherever I was meeting my friends, off came the sweater and out came the girl who just wanted to be able to wear what everyone else could, without being limited by seemingly outdated rules. "Here comes Sanj and her sweater bag. Let us know when we need to cover you," my girlfriends would laugh, throwing their unworried naked arms in the air, half-jesting a reality that wasn't real for them.

I laughed along; the tension removed with each arm that slipped out of the confines of a sleeve. I felt free like my exposed shoulders! I was wild like my stout, uncoordinated limbs!

Until I would inevitably run into an auntie who was a close friend or relative of my mom's and would probably give me a disapproving glare, I was fine. That one look would say so much about shaming my family and community while prancing around in public indecently exposed.

Well, you couldn't win them all.

CHAPTER 4

Mustache Girl

"WOW, I didn't know girls could grow mustaches!" Those smug words, uttered by a fellow classmate to my ten-year-old self, would affect my life up until this day. Just that morning when I left for school, I could only characterize myself as a slightly overweight, moderately quirky, very nerdy girl with fashion dreams.

Suddenly I became the girl... with a mustache!

I spent the entire school day asking to be excused from class to go to the bathroom and stare panic-stricken at the monstrosity on my face. I climbed up on to the sink, my breath fogging up the mirror, as I went slightly cross-eyed, turning my eyes into magnifying glasses. It seemed to be growing by the second, the hairs getting darker each time I inspected it.

When the bell rang at 2:15 p.m., I went straight home to mom and asked, nay demanded, that we run to the nearest waxing salon faster than the rate at which the hairs on my upper lip were growing.

She looked at me calmly and said, "What mustache? I don't see any hair."

I was flabbergasted. "This!" I screeched, pointing to the thing that looked like a black caterpillar resting on my lip.

Mom continued being coy, telling me I was imagining things and that nothing was there. In an effort to convince her, I positioned my fingers into makeshift tweezers and used all my might to yank out a whisker. "Look at this!" I wailed, delicately holding a strand of the thing I now hated the most.

She didn't budge and kept dismissing any existence of a mustache. For a moment, I actually believed her and decided that the moron from school needed glasses. I felt sorry for him because his parents probably didn't have time to take him to the eye doctor.

I went back the next day to my absolute horror, not only did he taunt me again, but also started a nickname for me.

"Mustache girl…"
"Mustache girl…"
"Mustache girl…"

For weeks I would run home, dramatically shrieking about my mustache, while my mom continuously said she couldn't see anything. At this point, I suggested that maybe she was the one who needed glasses, except she already wore glasses. She couldn't understand my plight anyway. She was one of the exceptions to the Indian woman's hairy curse. I'd never seen thick dark hairs anywhere on her clean, milky skin like the kind that grew out of my face, stomach, back, arms and legs.

One afternoon, when no one was around, I snuck into my parent's bathroom to find the thing that would save me, my dad's razor. I gingerly held it to the corner of my mouth, and just as I was about to wipe out "Mustache girl", I heard someone approaching and chickened out.

This happened almost every time and thus, the battle to wax dragged on for ages.

My mom's mustache denial tactic was not only her way of protecting me from the "womanly duties of hair removal", but also an important lesson in self-confidence, even if I didn't see it at the time. I would have my whole adult life to deal with waxing, threading, shaving, bleaching and plucking errant hairs. She kept warning me that as soon as I started the process, I would have to keep doing it, and it would require a lot of time and maintenance. She made it sound like once removed, a beard would grow between lunch and dinner, and I would have to tweeze every hour. She wanted me to focus on being a kid instead of my fuzz.

It's funny, I wasn't oblivious to the fact that I had a mustache. I knew I had one. I simply didn't care or know what it meant until someone else attached their negative connotation to it.

When you're the girl with the mustache, you can't control how others will judge you. Instead of being defined by your facial hair, you have to develop something else to make you intriguing. It's about learning and growing so that you become interesting in spite of your mustache, and that's what lasts a lifetime.

I cloaked myself in humor to deflect any negative comments that were thrown at me. What started out as false bravado eventually became genuine. The mustache could have grown so strong as to overpower me, push me into a corner to never speak up. However, it helped give me a voice and an identity.

"Wow, I wish my mustache was as thick as yours," prepubescent boys would cleverly say in their cracked tones.

"Yeah, and don't forget about my sideburns," I responded, feigning nonchalance.

I educated myself with American fashion magazines. No, I wasn't obsessed with trying to look like the athletic, pretty girl with straight hair and perfect skin, perpetually basking in summer all year long. I had no delusions of getting categorized as the smart and funny sidekick she befriends out of sheer niceness, perhaps even to copy my math homework.

A bonus of having these magazines was that it came with drool-worthy posters of teen idols of that time. I ripped out charming pictures of 90s heartthrobs to tape inside my locker when I entered middle school. Once while I was in class, another mean boy who loved to tease me and knew my locker combination opened it and drew a mustache on my posters with a ballpoint pen. I had to train myself to laugh it off when I first saw it and continued to ignore it whenever I needed to get my textbooks.

Undeterred, I studied what the girls on the pages wore. They appeared so natural, no matter their size, skin color or facial hair. Why couldn't a brown girl with a mustache achieve the same types of looks?

I tried every trend depicted in those magazines.

Chokers, glitter all around the face, flannel shirts tied around the waist, babydoll dresses, animal prints… I had absolutely no idea what my style was, what suited my body type, or how to dress appropriately for any occasion. I was merely an unfashionable furry sponge soaking up different types of looks much to the bemusement and sometimes horror of my parents.

It was important to experiment with my fashion identity as I learned how powerful clothes were in helping to quell my other insecurities. Everything I wore evoked more of a response than my mustache ever did.

The things I put on my body were received differently. It was either acceptable and inspiring to others, or offensive to one's sensibilities about how I was "supposed" to look. It didn't help that I had never been exposed to an Indian fashion education, as it wasn't as accessible and prevalent as the domination of Western clothing in Thailand. In Bangkok, people were cool and cosmopolitan, being Indian here was just a sidenote.

Baggy pants were all the rage in the 90s, although not Indian parent-approved due to their clownish and sloppy appearance. My mom despised it when the bottom of my oversized, extra-long jeans started tearing and fraying from being dragged across the ground — "Why are your pants mopping my floor?" she would jest, unable to understand why her daughter just wouldn't wear pieces that fit properly.

As clothes took over my identity, eventually my upper lip

fuzz became part of my face; after the initial teasing, nobody would comment on it again.

This was until my cousin, a fellow Indian who understood me, called one afternoon and told me she discovered a magical hair removal cream in her elder sister's bathroom cabinet. I sprinted as fast as my hairy legs could take me to her house down the street. Forget what anybody said about facial hair not being a big deal; if there was an opportunity to remove it, I was going to take it.

"Where's the stuff?" I anxiously asked, desperate to get a hit. My cousin led me to the bathroom, where the pink plastic tube sat seductively beneath the sink. I greedily squeezed it all over my fingers, feeling a tingle from each squirt of cream oozing out. The tingles pierced my face after I frantically smeared on half the tube, each burning sensation victoriously zapping the hair into nothingness.

It worked, but it also ended up scalding my skin into nothingness.

"What happened?" my parents asked when I came home, concerned but suspicious at the same time. "I tripped and hit my mouth by the swimming pool," I blurted too quickly, pulling my shirt over the tip of my nose and then further up to my eyes to wipe the tears of guilt, embarrassment and lingering pain. They gave each other a knowing look and walked away, shoulders slumped, their daughter testing the strength in their bones a little more each time.

I didn't dare look in the mirror as I got ready for school the next day. The last time I caught a quick glimpse of myself, I didn't have a mustache; I had a burnt caterpillar flaming above my lip. The possibility of earning a new, cruel nickname in the school halls was enough to keep me in bed, but the fear of my parents' wrath for my stupidity forced me awake. I ripped my navy-blue physical education t-shirt and shorts off the hanger, the ribbed neck of the shirt scraping my scabbed upper lip as I pulled it over my head.

"What happened to your mouth?" my friend asked, as she joined me on the bench while our classmates continued their aggressive game of volleyball.

"Nothing, I fell." The lie slipped out of my mouth again.

By that time, she was looking down at my feet. "Sanjana! Haven't you started shaving your legs, yet? My mom bought me a razor when I was eleven. You really need to start. Maybe, shave your arms too," my friend — or should I say "evil devil of a friend who would probably cause me years of therapy and insecurities later" — said, looking at me innocently with her small, beady eyes and stupid hairless body.

I would like to take this opportunity to thank the incredibly important people who have dedicated their time and energy to allow me to undergo numerous hours, months and years of hair removal.

Without you, I would be nothing.

CHAPTER 5

What Do You Want For Dinner?

I'M watching a movie with my friends on Friday after school. My cell phone rings. It's my mom. *Strange! I just texted her that I'm at the cinema and will be home later, why is she calling?*

Worried I may be forgetting an important family function and nervous that some auntie may have tattled that she saw me walking with a group of boys, I frantically pick up.

"Mom, I'm in a movie," I exasperatedly whisper. "I can't talk now."

"What do you want for dinner?" she replies, completely ignoring me.

"Mom! I don't know, can I call you later?"

"Just tell me what you want to eat for dinner."

"Mom!" I shriek, "I don't know! Don't ask me, I can't talk now!"

This exchange happened almost every day of my life when I lived at home with my parents. It wouldn't matter whether I was on a plane landing from an overseas trip or getting ready to accept a Nobel Peace Prize. My mom was on point to catch me any way she could to inquire what should be on the menu for that night.

She had long stopped asking my dad because he always gave the infuriating and unhelpful "Anything" answer. As a result, she would tackle my brothers and me one by one, until someone finally responded.

It wasn't exactly that we were picky eaters. It just seemed to be one of those Indian mom-things to pester her kids about food in any way possible. I supposed it is a mom's way of showing she cared. She probably asked us "What do you want for dinner?" more than she has ever asked "How are you?", "How was school?" or "Do you need to talk about your innermost fears and insecurities?"

However, her persistence regarding this question drove us all insane, especially as we got older and had more important things to do than think of what we wanted to eat five hours later.

Traditional Indian mothers structure their lives around their families. When one meal ends, you already have to start planning for the next. As we got older, our lunches started taking place at school or our workplaces, so dinners were the only time we were actually together as a family again.

Dinners are crucial for Indian families. Whether at home or the mandatory Sunday restaurant meal with extended relatives, everything is a shared experience. My father's biggest fear was his family turning into a disconnected bunch, where siblings stopped speaking to each other over arguments in the family business or daughters running off and leaving their parents behind. As we take our usual seats at the dining table, my dad would pass the rice and wisely remark, "A family who eats together stays together."

The first time I dined at a restaurant with my new non-Indian married family was a cross-cultural shock. Growing up with strong Asian influences, I was used to eating "family-style" where you order a bunch of dishes and share everything on the table. There's no such thing as ordering one main course per person. We order ten of them so we can all try a bite of everything!

I scanned the appetizers on offer at the Italian restaurant, unsure who would take the lead on ordering the food. When the waiter arrived, each member requested their own entrees and returned the menu. As he approached me, I panicked and quickly pointed to the first pasta dish listed as I hadn't even reached the main course section. I had been under the impression that we would all share a few starters as I was used to doing at my family dinners, before moving on to the next course. I wasn't trying to be greedy. I just wanted it to feel familiar. Clearly, they didn't possess the same ravenous appetite and penchant for gluttony as my Indian family.

My husband used this opportunity to order a steak, which is a treat for him. One part of my Hindu education that stuck with me was not eating beef, perhaps more because of fear than fact. I felt completely abandoned.

My dad's warnings about how marriage is hard rang in my ears. He had often asked me why I would make my life more difficult by marrying someone from a different culture. Was this what he was talking about? Did this mean I could never eat the way I truly wanted with my new family? Would my children learn how to share their food? Would I forever be hungry?

I left that meal with my in-laws, grumpy and conflicted. My husband thought I was being silly and said I should have just ordered something else. I asked him how I could do that since I was newly married and wasn't that comfortable speaking out yet. Plus, I would look high-maintenance and fussy (which I guess I am, but my new family didn't have to know that right away).

At my Indian family dinners, our table extends halfway across the restaurant due to the large number of relatives attending and no surface area is spared as dishes are brought out by the dozen. There are no restrictions on ordering as everyone has varied tastes. It may seem excessive but this way everyone leaves full and happy. No word on how neighboring tables feel about being seated next to our kooky and boisterous clan.

Even at home, my mom made sure the dinners would have no less than three main dishes as someone was vegetarian, someone was off carbs for a week and someone had decided they didn't want to eat anything yellow anymore. Perhaps we were spoiled for choice but that's also why my mom wanted to make sure we didn't complain when dinnertime actually came around (although we did anyway, because what else were ungrateful kids for).

Food and the way in which we share meals is a unifying force to our Indian heritage. Even if we dress or act outside the bounds of what our society prefers, at the end of the day there's always comforting *daal* (Indian lentil soup) and roti on the table.

I despised daal until I got married. Growing up in my parents' home we only cooked vegetarian food on Mondays and Tuesdays. Mondays we abstained from meat to honor Lord Shiva and Tuesdays were reserved for Lord Hanuman, according to my mom's decree. I would purposely plan to be out for dinner those days so I could eat whatever I wanted. Suddenly my new life away from my family was filled with so much uncomfortable newness and anxiety; daal became home for me.

Indian family dinners are chaotic, food is constantly being passed around. We talk loudly over each other, laugh at lame jokes, hear the latest gossip on so-and-so's drama and feel better that we are still here and together, no matter what happens beyond the table. Uncles argue over who is going to pay the bill with the "boss" of the clan winning every time. *A family that eats together stays together.*

My grandmother never broke a sweat in the kitchen even with hours over a hot stove. Her trusted companion was a stainless-steel tray of spices. Each compartment housing something orange-y red, mustard yellow and varying shades

of brown to create a burst of flavors that were unexpected of their drab, powdery and sometimes lumpy consistency; a small white plastic spoon with the handle strategically snapped off to fit perfectly with each spice bowl, used to season dishes with the know-how that only experience could provide.

During college my new American friends were excited by the possibility that I could cook them Indian food. Embarrassed that I didn't know anything, I called my mom to ask for the recipe of chicken curry and how to get my hands on that colorful tray of seasonings I always saw in the kitchen, still not knowing the names of any of them.

In trademark Indian-mom-style, she refused to share any tips, turning it into an opportunity to scold me instead: "See, don't you think you could have come into the kitchen and learned how to make some food instead of going out with your friends all the time and buying clothes. Now you don't know anything about your heritage, just wasted your life thinking about boys and God knows what nonsense."

I do miss the days when my mom used to call me and ask what I wanted for dinner.

CHAPTER 6

"What Will People Say?" *A Reflection*

WHEN you're a young and cute baby, your parents have full control over everything you do, your life is in their hands. Just look at old baby photos for proof of the nonsensical outfits layered with tulle and ruffles that they made you wear. Around the age of two your brain goes on alert and tells you that the best way to display a little bit of your power over them is to start throwing some major tantrums. Your caregivers now have to get crafty and try their best to balance your needs with their authority. From then on, the years are a constant push-pull between the child and the parents, each trying to exert dominance.

This is until finally something goes off in your teenage years that makes you fully break away. You're all grown up and independent — or so you think. You stop listening to your parents — or anyone for that matter. In fact, at this point, my

only style goal was to never dress like my mother. Her arms were always covered in long-sleeved, loose-fitting blouses, untailored pants hiding her slim figure and her skin so pale because it never saw the sun.

You start experimenting. Blue eyeshadow is a rite of passage that every teenage girl must try and fail at multiple times before it stops looking clownish. You begin testing more boundaries. The skirts get shorter and the sleeves disappear. Your innocent childhood friends are traded in for the cool kids, or become the cool kids themselves.

Your parents step in again, remembering a time they had full control. But it's too late. You have a mind of your own and there's no going back now.

They pull out all the stops to try to reel you in.

You play your favorite game each morning over breakfast: *Which relative or random auntie's daughter will mom compare me to today?*

Possible options include:

"You know Sangeeta is only 15 and she already knows how to fold her own samosas and make the most fragrant *sabzi*s anyone has ever tasted! She will have so many men lining up to marry her! What shopping nonsense do you do? Waste of time!"

"You know your cousin Rajeev…"

…Wait, what, I have a cousin named Rajeev?

"No, he's not exactly your cousin, don't be smart with me. You know, it's Auntie Sonia's son, from the nail salon. He's already studying to be a doctor. And you? Just idling away painting your face with all this red lipstick and green nonsense on your eyes. You want people to think you're a clown?"

"You know [insert anyone who is not me]. She is always so presentable and sweet. She does namaste and touches my feet every time she sees me. You just make a bad face and don't even talk nicely to anyone. What will people say?"

And there it is. Every (Indian) parents' greatest worry and threat uttered in one small phrase.

What will people say?

This all-encompassing fear can range from how you dress to who you love, from which school you attend to the profession you choose, from where you live to which car you drive, even down to how much milk you add to your chai. Everything and anything is potential for someone else — these hypothetical other "people" — to weigh in their opinions and judgments. If their perception of you is negative, this shame can travel back to sully you and your family's reputation. This is a rhetorical question that every son or daughter has had to hear in various forms, to varying degrees, for all sorts of offenses.

More often than not, the truth was that Sangeeta could only make delicious food because her parents found out she had a secret boyfriend and punished her by making her stay home and away from him. Of course, no one wanted to reveal that part of the story.

All my life decisions were put under the maddening lens of this nonchalant and vague jab. *What will people say?* Who are these "people" and why the hell do they take an interest in matters that are none of their business?

As a parent, this menacing line is used preventatively and as a means to ensure your child behaves the way they are supposed to, in line with the practices of the community you belong to: "You are staying out so late. What will people say?"

Growing up as an Indian promotes interdependence among families and society. It is the long-established norm for Indian kin to all live under one roof and to work in business together. There's no "moving out at 18" — daughters usually only leave when they get married and moms will use their last one per cent of phone battery to call their adult sons (and most likely ask what they would like to eat for dinner).

I grew up in the same house as my paternal grandparents and stayed close to all my relatives until this day. I don't differentiate between sibling or cousin — they are all one and the same to me. Even if modern families are choosing to live independently, the sense of closeness is still quite intact.

The issue arises when this connection is taken one step further and suddenly all our choices become communal. It goes beyond the confines of our nuclear family and travels to the watchful eyes and alert ears of others who may not even be relevant to the matter.

This highly-tuned Indian radar is programmed in aunties and uncles — no, not your actual relatives, just what we call the elder men and women of the society. These are the people whom our parents make us greet with a clumsy namaste even though we don't know who they are (but they *always* know who we are). They become one added layer of the people who are part of the choreographed "What will people say?" dance.

To add ghee to the fire, these aunties and uncles propagate the idea that there are really people judging you. One way in which they do this is with their penchant for staring. On the surface it comes off as being rude and nosy (which it is). But it also ties back to the idea of Indians being communal. You see, by staring at you, their brain is actually trying to compute who you are. In Indian communities overseas, such as ours in Bangkok, perhaps this skill is a survival mechanism to foster connections and closeness.

Their mind sifts through the database of Indians they know — once they realize who you are, they are able to compute what family you belong to, what your parents do for a living, the names of your grandparents, what village you descended from, where you live, how many siblings you have, what you ate for lunch. Oh, and of course they can recall any dirt on you and your family, perfect to use for gossip at their kitty parties.

But because they don't know anything about you as a person, they are only able to communicate with you on a superficial level by targeting your appearance or asking you questions that relate to what society expects of you.

The common comments that make recipients cringe:

"Wow, you've gained some weight."

"You've gotten so dark; you should apply some yogurt on your face."

"You're looking so tired."

"Don't you think you should put a shawl over that?"

"That's a bit short, isn't it?"

"When are you getting married?"

"Will you have children soon?"

"Will you have another child soon? How many are you planning to have?"

It's a shame no one ever thought to ask, "How are you?"

Our parents' reputation is only as good as their children are. A "successful" parent can be one that has raised a trained doctor, or as simple as having all their children be married (bonus points for being a doctor *and* married). No parent wants their children to bring shame upon their name or their standing in society. How a child acts also reflects upon their legacy as a whole, a concept deeply intertwined with Indian ways of living. So, we come back to the familiar warning: "What will people say?"

But of course, no one wants to say anything about their own story.

CHAPTER 7

Beti, Where's Your Lipstick?

I CAN'T count the number of beauty "rules" that were thrown at me as an Indian girl. They came from mothers, grandmothers, nosy aunties, strangers on the street — anyone who thought they knew better. It was a rare day that my appearance wasn't critiqued in some form, well-meaning as it was.

My grandmother couldn't hide her disdain for the way I presented myself. "Sanjana, your hair is not supposed to be covering your eyes. You look sloppy," she declared anytime she caught sight of me. I tried to avoid her as much as I could because I was more progressive than her superficial comments. Once in a while, I could hear grandma telling my mom, "Please show Sanjana the proper way of doing her hair, this is not how girls are supposed to look."

I was self-conscious tying it up because I was embarrassed about the thick sideburns that grew down the length of my face. At school, a few malicious kids who fueled my insecurity would call me "Mr. Burns", their clever reference to my sideburns. It wasn't as widespread as "Mustache girl" but it stung all the same. The only style I sported was leaving my disheveled hair down to frame my cheek so that it would hide my facial fur. It was a terrible look, and concealed nothing especially when the wind blew.

My grandmother continued to chastise me for having my hair in my face. She would compare me to the *bhabi*, the daughter-in-law who is often portrayed as a villain, on her Zee TV serial and remark on how young girls today have no shame and dress badly. "Pull your hair back in a tightly wound bun," she would say, pointing to her own midnight-black coif, spun like a perfectly circular charcoal *laddoo.* Secured with bobby pins in all directions, it was strictly parted down the center, and didn't have a single strand out of place.

"Grandma bun" wasn't exactly the look that I was attempting to master, and so, I never heeded her advice. Her generation was known for always maintaining neat hair, being smartly attired, wearing a full face of extra-light foundation that was never properly blended into the neck, coupled with a bold lipstick. This is mandatory even if they were just staying home and complaining to their maid about how watery their chai tastes.

This dedication to physical appearance was passed on to the next generation as evidenced by the number of aunties who keep their neighborhood hair salons thriving.

The same effort has appeared to be lost on "girls today" who are so daring to appear in public without makeup coupled with godforsaken things like having our raggedy hair in a man-bun, wearing tattered clothing and looking like we just rolled out of bed (because we did).

Despite it being a quick trip to the supermarket or a rogue hungover operation to search for some greasy food, nothing distresses the auntie's sensibilities more than seeing a young woman not making a little effort to spruce up her appearance. Their appalled response:

"*Beti,* you went out looking like that? Not even a little lipstick or blush-on?", they would say, referring to us using the Hindi term for "daughter" even though clearly no one would wish for any mother to say that.

Their mind swirls to nightmares of their precious sons having to one day endure the sight of a bare-faced woman showing off her ghastly pores and uneven skin tone. They wonder how we could even attract a man to begin with, if we're flaunting our dark under-eye circles and plain mouth.

Who could blame aunties for their horrified reaction? I mean, these are the same people whose biggest problem in a day can be that their dipping biscuit gets too soggy and breaks off into their tea. Many of them come from a generation where they always (and still do) have to look presentable for their husband and/or mother-in-law. And while a day can be more productive and positive when you look your best, I have no issues walking around my apartment complex with the building janitor better dressed than me.

There is already so much pressure on women to be perfect in all the roles we juggle — daughter, sister, wife, mother, daughter-in-law, employee, businesswoman, friend and house manager. Is it really a crime to enjoy a few extra minutes of sleep instead of putting on some lipstick and combing your hair?

Having this expectation to look made-up all the time devalues the many other things women are able to accomplish, even if we are wearing elastic sweatpants while doing it.

But there's no point trying to justify it as the criticism about appearances don't end. In fact, the requirements only seem to increase as you get older!

Aunties should trademark their own special brand of unsolicited beauty recipes, because it works every time:

*1 cup judgement

*2 pinches of outrage

*3 servings of impatience

*4 teaspoons of their preferred stereotypical horrified expression (my Punjabi elders preferred "*hai hai*" — an expression often used to show surprise or disappointment with a dramatic head shake)

Our Indian elders then turn to their most valued space — the kitchen — for solutions to every type of problem regarding your looks and health, whether you know it is a problem or not.

Haldi or turmeric is a staple in every Indian household. It is a mustard yellow spice added to the majority of Indian dishes touted for its digestive properties, anti-inflammatory benefits and less celebrated for its amazing ability to stain your clothes, fingers and countertops. It helps ease aches and will make your brain better-functioning, so you can finally bring home the stellar grades your parents demand of you. Whenever I developed a bit too much of a tan — frowned upon in a society that obsesses over lighter complexions as a sign of beauty — from going to the beach or walking outside in the scalding Bangkok sun, my dadi would order me to mix some turmeric and yogurt and smear it on my face to lighten the tan.

My grandfather swore by eating *tulsi* (plain basil leaves) every day to help with immunity. In the mornings, he would walk out to our garden and pluck two leaves. He chewed them raw like it was nothing, as if he was popping a piece of basil-flavored gum into his mouth.

"Your body is too *heaty*!" my Ayurvedic auntie would say whenever my face was a bit too flushed or I had a pimple pop up. "Eat cooling foods!"

I didn't really know what she meant by heaty; this word was thrown around a lot to diagnose any random ailment in the alternative medicine world. Is it bloating? Fatigued and irritable? Boyfriend broke up with you? (Just kidding, we all know Indian girls don't have boyfriends, we wake up married one day.) *"Heaty, heaty, heaty!"* My auntie later explained to me that heaty foods are those that can raise the temperature in one's body.

Of course, there is science behind the concepts of cooling and heaty foods. Fried foods, spices like ginger, meat and chocolate, are all believed to produce heat in the body. Heaty foods do have their beneficial moments of helping to improve circulation, eradicate colds and pump up the body. On the other hand, they are also known to cause excessive thirst, irritability, sore throat, fever and skin irritation.

Cooling foods can help to nourish oneself and rid the body of toxins, but both types of heaty and cooling foods should be in balanced proportions in the body for optimal health and functioning, according to sources that are more educated than me.

As a kid, I thought coconut oil was exclusively used for lathering your hair. Good Indian girls who listened to their moms had their hair braided with a generous helping of coconut oil every night and supposedly woke up with shiny, lustrous hair that never fell out or turned gray. On the contrary, I would go to bed with sopping, freshly washed hair; then wake up with a tangled rat-tail of a mess and a head cold from the combination of air-conditioning and wet strands. I only found out in adulthood that coconut oil could actually be used for other purposes like cooking or applied to your skin, not just greased on Indian heads.

My mom was wholly committed to soaking almonds every night and peeling off the skin for her precious children in the morning. It was a fixture on the breakfast table — glistening off-white *badaam* (almonds) next to our regular buttered toast and eggs. Apparently, the brown skin on the almond is difficult to digest; the peeled ones are better and "will make you smart". There were always a few extra almonds thrown into my bowl of cereal the morning I had an important exam or job interview.

In the few free moments she had during a day, my mom would be glued to the TV listening to sermons about health and wellness from spiritual pundits. She did a nightly check of her WhatsApp messages and forwarded us numerous tips like which points on the body to press to stimulate hair growth, or why you should never drink ice water. That's the thing about my mom — anything she learned became gospel to her and she applied it to her daily routine to safeguard her family's lives in the best way she knew how.

Our Indian elders do know what they're talking about to some extent with these notions, but it tends to lose its appeal when they take it too far and become pseudo-doctors, ready to tell you everything that's wrong with you inside by looking on your outside.

But while you're sipping your warm *jeera* water to lose weight or lathering yourself in home-made yogurt to become the right shade of white, don't forget — you still have to professionally style your hair and pretty up your face because, God forbid, what's the point of all of this if you are not able to land a husband!

CHAPTER 8

Degrees of Freedom

UNLIKE my mom's generation where attending a formal university was not considered a necessity for women, it was expected when my millennial time came around. While our mothers minted their role as newly married housewives and young parents, females in my peer group were able to explore their options, solely because we had more options. My parents didn't impose any restrictions on where I went to college or what major I chose to study. Their priority was making sure their children had earned a reputable degree at the end of it.

My parents agreed to let me go to university in a far-away land called America. It is a huge generational leap for Indian parents to trust their daughters by letting them leave home in a context other than marriage.

My father accompanied me before the start of my first semester to help me settle in. As an international student at an American college, my sheltered life became very apparent. My dad had to teach me simple things like how to make my bed, sort laundry and use a coffee machine, tasks that were never required of me at home where my existence revolved around school, friends, thinking about my clothes and getting in trouble for going out too much. It prompted much ridicule from my first American roommate who reminded me "there are no maids here" and openly complained about my lack of domestic skills on the phone to her mother while I was within earshot. I had grown up idolizing American culture, trends and fashion, but suddenly the everyday reality was so different from my privileged world. I had to fend for myself while gaining my first real taste of "independence" from a comfortable life under my parents' well-maintained and well-staffed roof.

It couldn't have been more different from my dad's experience. At the age of five-and-a-half, his parents sent him from Bangkok to a boarding school in Simla, where he would study until he graduated at 16. He laughed every time my overprotective mom coddled us and worried how we would fare when we had to fly back to college in America alone. "I was put on a plane and sent to India by myself as a kid. I had no choice. Surely our children can handle their own boarding passes," he chided her.

As the youngest of five siblings, my dad was the only one who was afforded the luxury to go to university abroad. Indian sons have the option to join the family business straight after finishing school but in his case, there were already too many family members working, so it was decided he could pursue further studies in the meantime.

My dad went to a university in Melbourne in 1977, at a time when there was a strict quota for the number of foreigners who could attend. Despite being offered more opportunities than his siblings, my dad always stayed grounded and remembered his obligation to his family. "I already had a path set out for me; the best thing I always did was listen to my parents," he reminded us whenever we questioned our predetermined plan. Upon graduating with a degree in economics and accounting, he returned to Bangkok to join the family textile business and dutifully followed through with his arranged marriage to my mom.

It was easy for my father to do what was expected of him with no defiance. He had seen the world and many of the possibilities that came with it. But he was steadfast in honoring the wishes of his family, choosing to do what he thought was right for the greater good than what served himself. It was as if these two concepts are mutually exclusive, that what an individual wants could not also be beneficial for the family. This was the root of all the battles I would fight in my life.

Our duty as Indian kids is to minimize any shame we bring to our good family name and make our parents proud, even though they will never explicitly tell you that. Our privilege expects us to get a good education, do right by our community, get married and have children all within a predefined timeline. Sometimes our conservative traditions cannot withstand all that we have learned and been exposed to, though.

My penchant for rebellion did make me bring home a few remnants from my time in college that did not fare well with my parents.

A few of the surprises I came back home with, ranking from *terrible* to *worse than life itself*, were: 1) An eyebrow piercing; 2) A lower back tattoo courtesy of a wild Floridian Spring Break vacation; 3) A white boyfriend.

I first saw him outside the building where my literature class was held. I was waiting with my friend for class to start when this tall, white, very non-Indian dude hobbled up on crutches (due to a basketball injury I would later learn). Not quite the entrance that would make a girl swoon. He clumsily balanced on his crutches to wave and greet almost every student who passed him, towering over all of them, while I watched wondering why his presence had suddenly caused my face to flush and my heart to race.

I didn't overtly come to college to find a lifelong partner but it was in the back of my mind. "Marry an Indian" was a mantra that had been instilled in me frequently since I was a child. So I assumed it was something that happened easily, that even if you explored other options in the meantime, there would be an Indian partner waiting for you in end. I knew of girls in my community who had met the perfect Indian doctor, lawyer or finance guy at university and moved abroad with them after marriage. It sounded so liberating — the possibility of relocating overseas and leaving behind a small-knit community with seemingly small-minded people, starting a new adventurous life in magical modern cities like New York or London. There, we could reinvent ourselves and live how we wanted without being held accountable to those who confined us. What better place to start looking for a suitable match than in this new environment?

There was a Rahul in my childhood psychology class who invited me to an off-campus party but then spent the whole night flirting with another girl. Another guy, Amir, started off nice but then never talked to me again when I refused to do more with him. Then there was Ishaan. But his friend warned me that Ishaan was just looking for a good time, so I was better off staying away from him if I wanted something more serious. I should have known that college men are usually what you think they would be, partaking in behavior that their mothers wouldn't be proud to know about. Perhaps they weren't ready to be locked down in relationships, as they knew they too would eventually have an Indian partner waiting for them in the end. Therefore, they were intent on using this time to have fun.

My chance encounters with the Tall Lad kept increasing in frequency, but that's perhaps because I started looking for him. My roommate who also happened to be my best friend, spent hours listening to me analyze and obsess over this crush I knew nothing about. One afternoon, she called me with glee in her voice. She informed me that the Tall Lad was in one of her history classes and she would make it her purpose to find out everything about him.

While we were sitting at a bar one night celebrating Wild Wednesdays, Thirsty Thursdays, or really any day which college kids use as an excuse to go out, the Tall Lad materialized from a constant fixation on my mind to physically coming through the entrance. My roommate jumped up and invited him to come and join us. He sat down at the tiny space remaining in the booth next to me, my shoulders barely reaching to his chest. The chatter and music around us deafened. My cheeks were so hot it could have melted the ice in my syrupy Tequila Sunrise. I could only feel the slight sensation of my roommate's foot kicking me under the table.

Later that night, he took my number. He even called me the next day and made plans to meet up again.

This would be the beginning of a relationship that would test every possible version of what I thought I wanted for my life versus what my family envisioned for me.

Dating the Tall Lad in college was easy. There were no parents I had to be wary of, no spying relatives and no aunties gossiping about us. Never once did a fellow college student look at us and think, "How could an Indian woman be dating a white man?"

If anything, our one-foot height difference was the most peculiar thing about our pairing. We could hold hands in public, show affection openly and eat at a restaurant together without worrying who would see us and what they would think.

Safeguarded by the college bubble, this was an experiment in full freedom. I could date any man I wanted. I had total control of how I presented myself. I could show up with anyone on my arm, even if that arm was left bare and uncovered without decent clothing.

My most daring online purchase during my first semester abroad was an army green tank top which was strategically shredded from the cleavage to navel area, perhaps to make up for the frayed tie-dye tank top I never got to buy with my dad when I was eight. I wore it out to college clubs and bars with my favorite shiny purple bra fully visible for everyone to see. This top never made its way into my suitcase back to my parents' house. There was no way it would survive in the laundry basket without a shrill screech from my mom. Was I a "bad" Indian for wearing this? Was I bringing shame on my family for indecent exposure? For the first time, neither was I plagued by these questions in my mind, nor did anyone care. This was America after all, the land of the free and that extended itself to a girl's bra.

Autonomy does not last forever for an Indian girl. No matter how untraditional or brave you think you are. Eventually the duties to your culture, gender expectations and family come knocking. Either you open the door and embrace it or keep it fully bolted to pursue your own path. There is no middle ground.

I kept the Tall Lad a secret from my family, although our relationship kept getting more and more serious throughout college. As graduation loomed closer, the reality of choosing him became more terrifying. With no job prospects in the US and the end of my student visa, I was due to return home to Bangkok. How would we stay together? How could I tell my parents about him? What had I been thinking when I made this decision? There was no way they would accept him as my partner or their future son-in-law.

I left America dumbfounded. I could hardly breathe on the airplane home. A never-ending stream of tears accompanied me on the long flight, along with a wet sleeve used to wipe my stinging eyes. The only respite was sleep, but the tears came again as soon as I would wake up, like a lucid nightmare reserved for those who are young and painfully in love. Walking into my parents' familiar house again was like nothing had changed. But four years of independence makes you different.

I called the Tall Lad my first night home, both of us experiencing so much heartache from this separation that we decided we couldn't call it quits. With emotions on high, we pledged we would do anything it took to make a long-distance relationship work until we met again. We video-called each other daily at crazy hours due to the 12-hour time difference. We emailed and chatted. I waited until my parents were asleep before I dared to talk to him. I was scared they would hear his voice emanating from my laptop speaker. If they were still awake, I would hide in my bathroom to talk.

Finally, the moment came! All those calls scheming about our meeting again and all the torturous waiting came to an end, when he flew to Bangkok to visit for a month. It had been about one year since I had left America and I still hadn't mentioned him to anyone in my family. I had booked a hotel room for him close to where I lived so I could meet him easily and discreetly. I warned him that I wouldn't be able to stay with him and we had to be careful about public displays of affection when we went out. I didn't know how to explain that it was immoral in my Indian society for us to stay together at the hotel, as it would tarnish my reputation, and my family's image.

It was normal in my world to come back to live with my parents but it wasn't right for a girl to be shacking up with a guy before she was married. The Tall Lad was upset and baffled, especially when he was coming all the way to Bangkok to see me after a year apart. He couldn't process it: "You're an adult woman with a college degree still living at home and you can't even tell them you have a boyfriend?"

He had known me as this free, independent girl with big dreams of perhaps one day being the editor-in-chief of a fashion magazine, maybe an investigative journalist for a prominent newspaper, or even the owner of a luxurious boutique. Now he saw another side — the girl conflicted with fear of disappointing her family and shaming her culture. He scoffed at my cowardice, which I had disguised as traditional values.

To make it up to him, I used part of my savings from my post-college job as an English teacher to book us a romantic three-night beach getaway on a beautiful secluded island, telling my parents it was a trip with my high school friends who had also returned to Bangkok from university. I also had the great idea to handwrite him a racy and romantic letter for each night of his stay in Bangkok to keep him "company", since I couldn't be with him overnight. I half-wrote the first provocative letter and left it folded haphazardly in my bedside drawer. "*I will never forget the first night when you walked into that bar...*"

After returning home from work one evening, my dad wasn't in his usual spot watching TV before dinner. He was in my room, his fists balled up over a piece of paper that quite visibly had my handwriting in blue ink peeking out. That perfect penmanship that my mom drilled in us as children, was now being used to compose filth. She stood next to my dad, with a look of disgust plastered on her face that made me want to take a shower and scrub all the sin off. My mom, who had no qualms about ever going through my purse or drawers, was holding a pack of birth control pills and the name card of the travel agency I had used to plan my beach trip.

"What is all of this?" my dad asked defeatedly, his otherwise youthful face stressed and fatigued. I was cornered. I confessed everything. I told them that I had a boyfriend from my time in college, he was coming to Bangkok and I would be going to pick him up at the airport in two days. I didn't confirm their suspicions about the birth control pills though, claiming they were prescribed by my gynecologist to help relieve my paralyzing period cramps, which was partly true. I couldn't put all these shocking revelations on my parents in one swoop.

They went into powerful parent protective mode. Emotionally charged threats starting flying around. *Don't let her leave the house! Take away all her money! Hide the car keys!* They knew all my devious plans now, and would sabotage it at every step. I didn't know what I was in for. The Tall Lad didn't know what he was in for either.

Neither of my parents spoke to me again for a while. My dad seemed dejected every time he saw me and my mom looked repulsed, but they didn't follow through on any of the threats they had made. On the night of the Tall Lad's arrival, I drove to the airport to pick him up overjoyed, sad and scared at the same time.

The Tall Lad and I met every day, but I still didn't dare stay the night at his hotel. I took him to see all the touristy sights — temples, markets, food stalls — far away from the Bangkok city center where the Indian community could easily spot us. He met all my childhood friends and their presence helped make his existence less jarring when we went out for dinners and explored the nightlife. If anyone saw us, I could easily pass him off as someone else's boyfriend.

After two weeks in Bangkok — with my parents giving me the silent treatment the whole time but not actually stopping me from going out — we were ready for our trip to the beach. Finally, we could get away from the city and enjoy our time together away from those who didn't want to see us together. No one in my home said anything as I took my suitcase, packed full of bikinis, shorts and tank tops and went to collect the Tall Lad from his hotel.

It seemed I would actually get away with this.

I had gone up to the Tall Lad's hotel room to meet him. Following all the rules I had set out for him in Bangkok was draining him as well. He couldn't wait to escape. Our relief was palpable as we got ready to go downstairs and get a taxi from the lobby to the airport.

"Was that a knock on the door?" the Tall Lad asked.

"I'm not sure," I distractedly replied, touching up my lip gloss. "Why would someone knock and not ring the doorbell? Did you leave the 'do not disturb' sign on?"

"Maybe they are just coming to check the minibar," he said.

I didn't think or bother to look through the peephole when I reflexively opened it.

There stood the face of my aunt, the one who always told me I was like her own daughter.

I slammed the door in shock and put the latch on. I ran to the bathroom in panic and dragged the Tall Lad with me. She continued knocking. What the hell was I supposed to do?

Could I leave my aunt waiting outside the door? How long would she stand there before she gave up and left? Was there another way we could leave the room without seeing her?

There was no escape. For fifteen minutes she kept on knocking. I mustered up the courage and let her in.

"Your dad asked me to come here," she began. "He is too hurt and disappointed to face you himself. Sanjana, you know what you are doing is wrong. You can't go on a trip alone with a boy. You are breaking your parents' heart," she trailed off, her face drained.

My parents had been very busy behind the scenes. All the while, I thought they had been letting me get away with my defiance. My dad had used his connections to find out the name of the hotel and room number that the Tall Lad was staying in. Using the name card she had found in my purse, my mom went to the travel agency and got a printed copy of my itinerary for the beach. My parents put together this information to send my aunt to catch me at the exact time I would be leaving. I was cornered.

"Please," I responded meekly. "We are going on a beach trip with my friends. There will be many other people there. It's not just us."

"Show me proof then. Let me speak to someone who is going on this trip with you," my aunt said.

No one picked up my calls or replied to my messages in time. It was a weekday during office hours. I was out of excuses. The beach trip was thwarted.

We didn't go.

My aunt left, proud of me for doing "the right thing". I glanced at the Tall Lad. He looked like he had been hit by a truck. In this case, my family was driving the vehicle full-speed ahead and it was headed straight for him.

CHAPTER 9

Brown and White Ain't Right

PERHAPS the biggest letdown for my parents was the fact that I didn't receive any marriage proposals once I became "of age". No one came forward to offer up their sons and I wasn't put in the running as a potential suitor for the children of family friends. My parents couldn't figure it out; I was well-educated, came from a reputable background and wasn't that terrible-looking in the right lighting. They thought Indian boys would be lining up around the block for me.

The only reason they could deduce was that my reputation preceded me. From the way I dressed, who my friends were, going out to parties at night, being outspoken about all my opinions and not being "Indian" enough — all these traits rendered me unsuitable for marriage, just like the black burn marks on an otherwise perfect piece of roti.

On top of it all, now I had a white boyfriend. My standing

in the community and chances for a good Indian life would be ruined once everyone inevitably found out.

It's funny that in the plight to protect their children, parents don't think about what they are doing to another person. The Tall Lad was a good and decent guy. But his lack of Indianness would be the driving force that my parents used to keep us apart. The question no longer became whether my Indian family could accept him — it was whether he wanted to be part of a relationship where people rejected him before they had a chance to get to know him. These factors would all lead to our eventual downfall.

His skin color wasn't the only problem. Not being Indian translates to so many other incompatibilities. It was presumed that he wouldn't have the same family values as us. He probably had one cousin that he wasn't close to, while we regarded our kin as blood. He would think it was OK to address my parents by their first names instead of the respectful "auntie" or "uncle". He was so tall he would have trouble bending down to touch my grandparents' feet as a sign of respect, let alone understand the significance of this custom. Marriage wouldn't be sanctified to him the way it was to us. This must be the reason why divorce was seemingly so rampant in the Western world, his own parents contributing to this statistic.

I trusted that we shared the same values, but it didn't matter. In the long-term how could we last without the support of either of our families?

Aunts, uncles and elder cousins were all called in to try to talk some sense into me. No one from outside the family was consulted because my parents couldn't bear the shame of letting them know it was their Sanjana who had got it wrong. "Remember what happened to Priya when she married Brian?" they recounted. "What has her life become now? Her parents barely attend any more social events, the humiliation is too much for them. It just doesn't work."

It didn't matter if I countered it with Indian unions that ended in divorce. No, in those cases there was always something wrong with the girl or her family and it didn't help to support my cause.

"You watched too many Hollywood romances," they continued, all preaching from the same line of thought. "But love isn't the only thing that makes a marriage work. Love can come later. Don't make it harder on yourself by choosing someone from a completely different background."

That's the funny thing — I had been around "Western" concepts my whole life from language to clothes to education, so it didn't feel completely different to me. In fact, I still need English subtitles to understand a Bollywood movie. But those who knew better were certain that these would be the nuances that would break us.

Contrast that to the advice the Tall Lad received from his family: "If you're happy, we're happy."

The warnings kept coming.

"You will not be able to maintain your comfortable lifestyle if you live independently. At least if you marry an Indian, they might have a family business to fall back on and numerous relatives for support."

"How can you survive alone in a foreign country? There they live paycheck to paycheck, and eventually you will get divorced or run back home."

"We are telling you now, we will not let you come back home if you choose to stay with him."

The assumptions were loaded, the statements were distressing. No matter the outcome there would be some degree of unhappiness for everyone involved.

For seven long years, the Tall Lad and I kept an on-again, off-again long-distance relationship going. We met in person occasionally during that time, but every visit was tinged with the reality of what we were fighting against. There were highs of believing we could make it and dreams of giving up everything to be together. There were lows of breaking up because the strain of not physically being in the same place was too taxing. Through it all, my family continued showing their unrelenting disapproval.

On and on the struggle kept going.

Finally, the frustration of neither of us making a choice to be together became too much. He wanted me to move to the US to be with him and get away from the voices that were keeping me down. I said he was asking me to sacrifice everything while he would give up nothing.

Part of me was too fearful about what would happen if I chose him. I was scared that the menacing threats would come to life. Nothing felt certain anymore and I went through every day in a daze, only the emptiness in my stomach reminding me that I could still detect pain. It came down to this: disobey my parents and take the uncertain chance of finding out for myself if a life with the Tall Lad would have a happy ending.

How could I be so nonconformist and bold in other parts of my life but still end up becoming the cowardly person I was rebelling against? I suppose the thought of losing one's family, and one's safety net, is enough to keep even the most headstrong person down. Maybe at the end of the day, I couldn't deny all the Indian-ness that ultimately defined me.

After seven long years, we exchanged our last defeated email, saying our final goodbye.

I had gone out with my friends that night to numb the end of a relationship that consumed me for most of my twenties. We had broken up a few times before, but I knew this time, it really was the end. I sat on the sidewalk in front of a bar with my phone in hand, typing out a very lame "wish you all the best" that summed up nothing about what we had been through together. I pressed the *Send* button.

I looked down at my black and white snakeskin flats, light wash denim shorts and gray crop top with a navy star printed on it. The sweater I had used to cover up my midriff-baring shirt so I could leave my parents' house, was spilling out of my purse. I hadn't bothered to hide the fact that I was wearing shorts outside. I walked right past my mom as I left the house, bare legs in plain view, every step conveying that I just didn't care anymore. Nothing mattered if I didn't have the one thing that completed an Indian woman — a good Indian husband.

That very night, whether through fate or my desire to prove I had learned nothing, I met someone — the non-Indian who would eventually become my husband.

The cycle began again.

CHAPTER 10

Swiss Miss

YOU know how it goes — you're told to avoid boys your whole life until you hit a certain age, and then your parents start freaking out about why you're not married yet.

Your mom frantically calls the pundit to check if your astrological stars have misaligned, and then sets up numerous pujas to remove any obstacles preventing you from marital bliss.

Aunties boast about their single successful sons, citing triumphs such as "You know he has his own car" or "My Rohit works for the top company in the UK", even though you know from social media Rohit's only achievements range from partying to playboying.

The buffet line of every wedding you attend is filled with concerned elders asking, "When's your turn?", making you dash to the bar instead. Say goodbye to your chances of finding a suitor because who wants a girl who drinks vodka all night to avoid being reminded of her single status?

Alas, the road to marriage can be a long and complicated one.

Some families are very strict with their spousal criteria; the mate should be from the same region in India, have a similar background, share religious beliefs, eat the same type of vegetarian food, follow the same gurus and the list goes on.

My parents believed such detailed requirements were not realistic given the diversity of people I would be exposed to in my international upbringing, thus they only had one request: the guy I brought home should be Indian. Well, technically their other request was for me to not bring home any boys at all but I guess I could have shown them a photo of any of my potential love interests.

It didn't matter if the guy was tall or short, Sindhi or Gujarati, non-vegetarian or even a beef eater, he just had to be an Indian. That's all — Indian.

It seemed so simple. Surely in this world with my home base in Bangkok, going to the US for college and connections on almost every continent, I would be able to find one suitable Indian man that would be my husband.

Does Swiss-Chinese count as Indian?

I don't know how I got so far off with my geography but somehow my fate led me to a man that would push my relationship with my family to the edge again.

My mom bemoaned what terrible karma she had accrued that made me turn out this way. My dad regretted how I took advantage of all the liberties he had given me. We were all just recovering from the turmoil I caused with the Tall Lad.

"What will people say?" was the resounding wail heard from all corners of my house.

My parents went through a checklist of everything they could have done wrong — letting me have sleepovers, the influence of my non-Indian friends, permitting me to leave the house at night, sending me off to America for college, the way I dressed, how I wore my makeup, drinking embarrassing amounts of Long Island iced teas, giving me too much freedom, not going to the temple unless I was forced to, the fantasies I conjured by watching too many Hollywood love stories, not grooming me to be Indian enough… basically everything that allowed me to be an independent girl with a mind of her own.

The Swiss-Chinese individual causing all the controversy had attended the same international school in Bangkok as I did; but with him being a few years older, we had only met through mutual friends when I returned to Bangkok after college.

Now that I was single again, my weekends were not spent in front of a laptop pining for a man behind the screen. I made more plans to go out and suddenly this guy that I had never seen in my life kept showing up everywhere. The more I saw him, the more I craved his company.

At a bar one night, the music suddenly stopped playing. I looked around to see the DJ packing up and the lights turned on. My friends had all disappeared and Mr. Swiss-Chinese was the only person I recognized, folding his change neatly into his money clip and taking the last sip of his whiskey. "Hey, do you need a ride home?" he asks me.

My cheeks start to flush. The now brightly-lit space showed littered remnants of the night's revelry and unmasked my feelings for him that I wasn't prepared to deal with.

"Do you want to go somewhere and have one more drink?" I replied, never ready to go home and always trying to keep the night going as long as the bars stay open. It was easy to do that in Bangkok where nightlife was part of the city's draw, and after-hours spots were readily accessible.

We sat at a makeshift roadside bar crafted from a "wagon" where the drinks were served in small buckets with multiple straws inside, intended for a group to share. Drunken partygoers clumsily walking down the street and fumes from taxis waiting to pick up passengers served as our very romantic backdrop. We drank an extremely potent Long Island iced tea crafted with cheap hangover-inducing alcohol from a red bucket, laughing about where all our friends had gone.

When the rickety plastic stools and sidewalk chaos became too uncomfortable, we walked down the road to a nearby late-night club. Packed with people who also weren't ready for the night to end, I told Mr. Swiss-Chinese that I was sure he would find a nice girl here. He gave me a funny look and squeezed his way to the crowded bar to get us some drinks.

I was oblivious to the fact that my mobile phone had been vibrating in my purse for quite some time. When I pulled it out to check, I saw about 60 missed calls from my dad.

"DANGER! DANGER!" flashed all over my screen. That might sound excessive but I hate to admit — it was standard practice when I stayed out too late and didn't respond to his texts.

I messaged my dad that I would be home soon and put my phone away. Mr. Swiss-Chinese came back with a vodka-cranberry for me and we sat in the corner joking about the shady characters that were present in this sleazy club, excluding ourselves of course. He took a small sip of his drink and always put the glass on the middle of the table avoiding its chances of being knocked over. I watched the intentionality of his actions; how considerate he seemed when doing such simple things even in this crazy club.

My phone started ringing again and when I pulled it out, I was brought back to reality by the time displayed on the top right corner: 4:47 a.m.

I panicked. It certainly wasn't my first time staying out late but I didn't feel like dealing with a lecture from my parents when I had been having such a great night. It was also early Sunday morning, so I knew the chances of running into my father leaving home to make his tee time at the golf course were high.

Mr. Swiss-Chinese accompanied me to a cab as the sun was rising. He told me to message him and let him know I got home safely. I had butterflies in my stomach throughout the whole taxi ride back to my house. They quickly flew away when I saw the angered look on my dad's face as I tried to dash up to my room without being seen.

"Who was the boy?" my dad yelled after me to no avail. I didn't know what was worse — being caught staying out late or being intercepted coming home in the crop top and denim shorts I was wearing after staying out all night. I quickly locked myself in my bedroom and went to sleep to avoid any further interrogation.

When I inevitably faced my parents later that evening, they treated the incident the same way they always had — with cold, disapproving looks about my behavior and the most agonizing silent treatment.

I tiptoed around the tense day, trying my best to stay out of sight by hiding in my room and sending flirtatious messages to my soon-to-be beau.

He invited me to go on a proper first date the following weekend — well "let's hang again soon" he casually said, but I quickly rephrased his text to confirm that I would be happy to see him again the following Saturday for a fabulous dinner that he would have the privilege of planning.

I had no idea if he would stay in my life as an acquaintance or if this would actually become something serious. I was in my late twenties and had moved on from my first job as an English language teacher to earning the title of editor at a local lifestyle magazine, a position that could only get me further in my career. However, I had no promising prospects in my personal life. Did I really want to pursue someone that my family might not be happy with, or worse, disown me over? I had just been through the same nightmare with the Tall Lad. Would I be happy in the long-term with someone from a different culture? Would our future kids suffer by not having a solid identity?

As my brain naturally began to overthink and overanalyze, Saturday came around and Mr. Swiss-Chinese decided our date would involve him cooking dinner at his place. He lived by himself, so his apartment was the perfect base for a private escape. He effortlessly cooked up some rigatoni pasta with sausage and mushroom, cleaning up as he went. Everything was so simple for him that being in his presence made me forget the imminent storm that was brewing outside these walls.

We continued to see each other more frequently. Every time I went out with him I would tell my parents I was meeting a different friend, drawing random names of anyone I had ever encountered. Either I was the most popular girl or I was attracting more suspicion toward myself.

One late night when I was with Mr. Swiss-Chinese at his apartment, my phone ran out of battery. "Your charger doesn't fit in my phone!" I cried, as I fumbled to force the silver square into the charging port, knowing full well it wouldn't work because we used different phone models. With no other option, I texted my dad from Mr. Swiss-Chinese's phone and wrote that this number belonged to my friend's older brother, and that I would be home soon.

I thought I was being responsible. But obviously, it was an amateur mistake. My mom immediately called the number. I was filled with fear as I saw my mom's number on the screen and I begged him not to answer. He didn't, but then it went to voicemail which clearly stated his name and asked the caller to leave a message — it definitely didn't mention the fake name that I had used!

When I arrived home later that evening both my parents were waiting for me.

"Who is he?" they asked again.

I told them the truth and that I really liked him.

"If you stay with him, you can expect nothing from us," they warned. They weren't joking. For two years, I was an unwanted, freeloading tenant who left home early each morning only to return to sleep at night. For two years, my parents didn't speak to me and I might as well have been invisible when I was around. For two years, I chose happiness with Mr. Swiss-Chinese, while dealing with fiery anger and resistance from my family.

CHAPTER 11

A Trip Down the Fiery Aisle

IN the two years that Mr. Swiss-Chinese and I dated, my father took it especially hard. He exhibited his stern disapproval of this relationship through silent treatment, blatantly ignoring me. He wasn't kidding around. He was giving me a harsh preview of what it would mean to be completely cut out of the family and sever all ties with them.

Dinnertime at home was particularly painful, in the rare moments that I chose to be present. If dad needed a dish that was placed right in front of me, he would ask someone else to pass it. It was an excruciating strategy to get a curry without having to face his daughter.

A family that eats together might not always stay together.

I spent all my weekends out of the house with Mr. Swiss-Chinese. No one overtly cared anymore if I showed up to family obligations, nor did they bother to inform me of any events. This anger trickled down to my brothers who blamed me for being selfish, and not being considerate about all the stress and grief I was causing my dad. My home became hostile to me, and I myself was the culprit.

In my father's eyes, he had given me everything growing up and I tested his limits at every turn, somewhat ungratefully. He had adapted his own beliefs as much as he could to subdue his defiant daughter. But one belief he couldn't let go of was that marriages end badly when two people are from different backgrounds. He couldn't imagine how a non-Indian family would understand the many rituals we abide by, how they could contribute to all the age-old traditions involved in a Hindu wedding, what place they would have in our Indian community and where I would fit in to all of this. He wanted me to have the best life and future, but that would never happen with someone who didn't come from the same culture. To make it even more confusing, now I was dangling someone who was also the product of two different cultures.

I didn't base my entire identity on being Indian. I couldn't rely on my ethnicity to make what would be one of the most important decisions of my life. I wasn't the only Indian at my multicultural school in Bangkok which had students from all over the globe. I wasn't the only Indian in my diverse college in America. Being Indian only mattered in my family, in a group of people whose names you might never hear about, but who loomed so large and so powerful in my world.

My choices wouldn't solely affect me — its impact would reflect on everyone in my family — grandparents, aunties, uncles, cousins — as a whole. My actions could tarnish our reputation and standing in our collective society, a society that wasn't ready to accept the ripple effects of change. Gossip was prevalent and common, and the juicy information could spread easily in any social gathering: *"Did you hear that Payal's niece wants to marry a Chinese guy? I heard he was from Spain or something. That's Anandji's granddaughter, right? Oh! I feel bad for her poor mother."*

The only way to end the unfairness would be to end the relationship. But this time I didn't back down.

I withstood the two years of silent treatment by staying mostly locked up in my bedroom when I was home. Yes, of course, I still lived with my parents! We, Indian daughters, don't move out until we get married and that was one rent-free aspect of my culture that didn't bother me.

At extremely low points when the silence became deafening, I would break free from my room and burst into uncontrollable tears.

"If you are so against all my relationships, why don't you just arrange my marriage to any Indian guy you want?" I would shout.

Equally hurt, they attacked back, "Who would want to marry you now?"

This went on and on for two long years, with both my parents and I refusing to budge.

Growing up, when my parents would talk to me about marriage, they always reminded me, "There's no guarantee about anyone. You just make it work." They could see I was losing myself to a fantasy world. To them, getting married was just something you did like waking up and getting dressed. It was a duty to be completed, a rite of passage for every son and daughter. It didn't matter which brown face was at the end of it. "Love-shmove" was a nonsensical concept that didn't ensure whether a couple would endure the test of time. Part of being a favorable Indian adult was seeing a bright future with anyone who seemed decent on paper and came from a respectable family.

Although their perspective on marriage was not unique to Indian parents, their own match had a degree of rarity — my father was betrothed to my mother from infancy. My dadi and *nani* (maternal grandmother) were friends as they belonged to the same community in Bangkok. My nani, very much a byproduct of the entrenched Indian patriarchal system, believed she had failed her duty as a wife when her firstborn turned out to be a girl — my mother. My dadi soothed her letdown by offering my father to her in marriage. He had been born the year before my mom — "he will be your son one day as well" she promised my nani.

My dad always knew there was a woman out there that he was supposed to marry when he grew up — and was teased incessantly about it by his siblings during his childhood. But he only met my mother face-to-face when they officially got engaged at their ring ceremony. The "dating" began only after they were engaged. My dad would pick my mom up at her house, respectfully meet her parents inside, take her out to a restaurant for dinner and bring her back home at a very reasonable hour.

This was nothing compared to what I put them through.

All the men I dated were in secret, but of course my parents always found out about them anyway. Society's watchful eyes and big mouths, along with my own missteps for daring to go out in public with my latest flings, made it inevitable.

I kept the romantic parts of my life hidden because I knew my parents wouldn't approve or understand. We didn't talk openly about dating or relationships. It's as if we were never supposed to. Skip all the sex education and partnership conversations, and jump straight to getting married with our only knowledge being what we learned from TV and naughty friends.

My parents laughed about the first real heartbreak I ever experienced. Not quite the sympathetic response you would expect. I had come home from school unable to suppress the sobs when my senior year high school boyfriend (another non-Indian guy, no less) casually and cruelly decided he didn't have time for a girlfriend anymore, only to walk the halls with a new girl almost immediately. I cried through dinner and into the night. I couldn't bring myself to go to school the next day as my tears wouldn't stop and I could barely open my eyes because of how puffy they were. My mom couldn't believe I missed a day of school because of a silly boy. She ridiculed my weakness.

"I didn't send you to get an education so you could waste it holding hands with boys," she sternly scolded me.

Despite the fact that I shouldn't have even had a boyfriend, my parents were bewildered by concepts such as "taking time to get to know someone" or "finding ourselves before committing to a relationship." Break-ups didn't make sense to them; no one is perfect and the point of being with someone, anyone for that matter, is to make it last forever despite any obstacles. For them it was as simple as fulfilling the age deadline for getting married and listening to your elders about who is best for you (and them). They couldn't understand or see the point of drama that came with relationships because they had never experienced it with anyone else besides each other.

I countered their stance at every chance I got and retorted, "Well, I'm an independent woman and I can make my own decisions about who I am best suited to share my life with."

That only gave way to more rebukes about how people had way too much freedom and had lost sight of the values that really mattered.

My parents never referred to each other by their names. For the longest time, I actually thought my dad's name was "Listen" (*"suniye"*) because that's how my mom addresses him when she needs his attention. "Listen," she would say from the other side of the room, a simple word that would summon him, but that also conveyed the deep respect and deference a wife has to not call her husband by his name.

My relationship with Mr. Swiss-Chinese kept growing in the background. "Listen," I heard my mom utter often in a hushed tone from outside my locked door. "What are we going to do about Sanjana?" In those moments, I questioned my actions and wondered if I should just give up. How could I continue on like this seeing the hurt it was causing my parents? But the fighter in me couldn't bring myself to end it with him just because he wasn't Indian.

On and on the struggle kept going.

One April day, almost anticlimactically, my father approached me and broke the silence. He agreed to meet Mr. Swiss-Chinese. I was to set up a dinner on Friday night. He didn't say anything further.

I began hyperventilating. I called Mr. Swiss-Chinese right away. *Did he understand what this meant? Was he ready to meet my parents? Did he know he was now required to marry me? If he met my parents and broke up with me, did he realize he would further ruin my not-so-good name and I might lose any chance of ever getting married?*

He laughed. He was strangely calm, and uncomplicated. Nothing rattled him, not even the thought of being the one who would destroy generations of tradition.

The night of the dinner arrived. We met at an Italian restaurant which was always bustling with patrons, so any awkward silences wouldn't be pronounced. Mr. Swiss-Chinese greeted my parents with a namaste as I had instructed him to do, so he could make a good first impression. "Just show them you know some Indian stuff," I pestered him.

My dad got right into it. "I have had a lot of trouble accepting this relationship," he said to Mr. Swiss-Chinese. "You are not the person I imagined for my daughter. But she seems very sure that she is making the right choice."

Mr. Swiss-Chinese listened as my dad listed off all the reservations he had about us being together. "It is not your fault; I was not trying to attack you. This is how I was raised in my Indian culture so I don't know any different. And Sanjana has given me a lot to think about," he semi-apologized to Mr. Swiss-Chinese.

I was shocked. My dad went on to explain all the work he had been doing behind the scenes while I was carelessly running off to brunches, dinners and parties. Unable to find peace on his own, he was able to put things into perspective after seeking counsel from a Hindu pundit at our temple. Other parents in our community who had lost daughters to non-Indian mates spoke to my dad about their experiences, how they managed to deal with it and eventually accepted it. When he realized we wouldn't be outcast for bringing in a non-Indian into our family, he was able to have a slight change of heart.

"Sanjana has always forced me to see things differently," my dad continued to Mr. Swiss-Chinese. "Since she was a girl, she wore everything we forbade and did everything we told her not to do. But now we were worried she would ruin her life."

I admired my dad for giving me an honest chance and chipping away at his own cemented convictions for the happiness of his daughter. He put in the hard work of changing himself and his beliefs which wasn't easy for anyone to do.

The pain the last two years gave us instantly faded away like it never even existed.

"Now, are you sure your intention is to marry her?" my dad asked Mr. Swiss-Chinese. They clinked their beer glasses in agreement and the dinner reached its resolution. Tensions began to thaw at home.

At intermittent points, my dad would still ask me if I was sure about my decision. I told him that Mr. Swiss-Chinese may not be Indian but he respects his elders, considers the well-being of his family and is responsible with a strong work ethic. What could be more Indian than that? "You will see that for yourself," I assured my dad.

On the weekend of my 30th birthday, my family and I were happy again. To mark this milestone, we planned a celebratory trip to Siem Reap, Cambodia, only a one-hour flight away from Bangkok. It was understood that Mr. Swiss-Chinese couldn't join a family trip because we weren't married yet. I met him for dinner the night before I left, for an early birthday celebration.

When I arrived in Cambodia, I texted him to see how he was and what he was doing back in Bangkok. He said he was going to have lunch with his mom and would probably meet some friends that evening. "Wish you were here," I messaged back.

In the meantime, my family and I explored the city and took in some sights. Being with my parents on vacation reminded me of when I was a child, before life got messy and complicated. As the evening approached in Siem Reap, we went back to the hotel to freshen up before dinner. Siem Reap's climate was similar to Bangkok and I didn't expect to be having any late nights on a family trip. Keeping that in mind, I had only packed very casual clothes on this trip. Besides, I decided to give my skin a break from makeup because I didn't need to impress anybody around here; so, I didn't bring any.

My elder brother and his wife were also on this trip. They had gotten married in the midst of my drama with Mr. Swiss-Chinese. My sister-in-law came to my room while I was getting ready. "Are you sure you don't want to change your outfit?" she asked. "I think dinner is at a nice restaurant."

"I just want to be comfortable," I said, tucking my t-shirt into sweatpants and then pulling it out again. My sister-in-law went to the clothes half hanging out of my suitcase. "What about this blue dress? It's a nice color on you."

"I don't want to wear a dress today. Traveling makes me feel bloated," I stubbornly insisted. She smiled and adjusted the hem of her own dress. "You look great, but I think you will feel better if you change," she said, cautiously and sweetly.

It wasn't like her to tell me what to wear. Finally, I agreed to put on the royal blue maxi dress. She went to her purse. "Here, you can use some of my lipstick too, it will match nicely." She pulled off the cap and twisted up a baby pink shade. "No lipstick!" I said.

We went down to the hotel bar for some pre-dinner drinks and snacks. Located just off the lobby, we all sat together on one couch. As I was looking through the drinks list, I caught a glimpse of someone walking in out of the corner of my eye.

How strange, I thought. *That waiter looks exactly like Mr. Swiss-Chinese!* I looked down at the menu again, and looked up, unsure if I was imagining things. That "waiter" kept walking towards me and got down on one knee. He pulled out a velvet box. All I heard was, "Hi" and "Will you marry me?" My ears had stopped working for a few minutes and I didn't process anything he had said in between. A diamond ring flashed from his hand and all noise around me stopped. In the periphery, I saw my dad pull out his phone. A message flashed on my screen: "Sanjana is engaged!" sent to the family chat.

My phone started flooding with congratulatory messages. "Wait, let me say 'yes' first!" I said, still in shock from the surreal experience. My sister-in-law handed me her lipstick and laughed. "Will you use it now for the photos at least?"

I found out that Mr. Swiss-Chinese had been planning this whole surprise with my father. They had been scheming about the best way to orchestrate this proposal to completely catch me off-guard. Mr. Swiss-Chinese had taken a later flight to Siem Reap the same day we left and was just down the hall from me in the same hotel.

I had read and watched many love stories. But in this love story, it wasn't the size of the diamond or the romantic setting. It was that this proposal brought my family together. Now Mr. Swiss-Chinese had been accepted into it.

I was able to enjoy being engaged for exactly one day and a half before our wedding preparations started in full swing. What I wanted to be a midsize pudgy ceremony, completely went out of my control into a big fat Indian wedding. Mr. Swiss-Chinese and his family gracefully came along for the ride, dispelling any fears about their integration into our Indian customs and (sometimes) craziness.

All my numerous relatives got involved with their opinions on every detail from what I should wear, how many parties we needed to have and who we should invite.

We had five days of the full-blown Indian wedding experience, while our actual marriage ceremony took place at a Hindu temple in Bangkok. I surprised even myself when I realized, I wanted to be the traditional Indian bride on my wedding day. This is the same girl who rejected her childhood religion classes, slept through Hindi lessons and never fully embraced her Indian-ness.

As I sat under my *mandap* — an altar which is constructed and beautifully decorated for Hindu weddings — with Mr. Swiss-Chinese next to me in his sherwani that matched my lehenga in shades of cream, gold and red, both our parents on either side of us, tears rolled down my cheeks. I didn't understand any of the Sanskrit vows being chanted, but every word resonated with me. I looked at the sacred fire burning in front of us. I was marrying out of my family into a different culture, but here I was — the most Indian I had ever felt in my life.

CHAPTER 12

The Married Woman's Code of Conduct

As I fumbled to pack away my heavy wedding lehenga, carefully laying the red *dupatta* on top, I could feel a weight lifted. The judgmental journey that plagued much of my single life was seemingly over.

After I got married, there was a collective sigh of relief among my parents. I was 30 at my wedding, extremely old in Indian years. I should have been welcoming grandkids at that point if I adhered to society's unrealistic chronology. But I was just one of those silly modern girls wasting my youth, trying to advance in a life that did not involve Roti Making 101 or obsessing about finding my perfect match.

My parents had been open to a modern compromise to traditional arranged marriages. Their friends told them that these days it's better to have an "introduction" where parents play matchmaker and try to set up their kids for a casual meeting such as a coffee date. Both parties have to be in agreement before any major decisions are made.

As we received wedding invitation after invitation, each more extravagant and gaudier than the last, my parents began getting nervous. Peers of my age group were all getting married while I had no prospects in sight. Suddenly everything I did became a reason no family was interested in having me marry their son.

"How come no one has approached us for you?" was the disappointed phrase my family kept reminding me of.

I had acquired a fun reputation of being known to have a bit too much to drink at other people's wedding sangeets, often seen shoeless, passed out inebriated on a chair with my bindi stuck on my cheek while the festivities continued around me. I was known to stay out late with good friends who all shared a penchant for enjoying one too many bottles of wine during happy hour and I had no problem vocalizing my radical opinions to any auntie or uncle who asked me the wrong questions at the wrong time.

It didn't help that society knew about my previous failed relationships with non-Indian men. "I don't want to marry any of these boys anyway, they're all spoiled hypocrites," I would announce anytime I had the chance, referencing the fact that they also went out, partied and dated around but wouldn't want to seriously settle down with a girl who did the same. It didn't matter what I said; each time, as a female, the critical finger was pointed back at me for what I was doing wrong to drive potential suitors away. It's not easy being a woman in an Indian man's world.

Now I was married. Not because I was pressured to, not in the way anyone expected and certainly not to the person they envisioned for me. But it also came with many bonuses for my reputation.

Not being married leads to so many more questions and judgments. We all know that one single elderly auntie who lives alone with no husband or children; we have more curiosity about her single status than understanding. The assumptions are usually negative; her family couldn't pay a dowry, her parents don't have a good standing in the community, she wasn't pretty enough to be a bride, she brought scandal upon herself.

I wonder how many of these women chose to follow their career dreams. Perhaps, they didn't find anyone they felt was exceptional enough for them. Maybe they were happier staying single and enjoying their freedom. Those thoughts probably didn't cross anyone's mind automatically, right?

Now my parents didn't have to worry about me scandalizing myself in society. My dad wouldn't have to stay up late and endure sleepless nights waiting for me to come home, then play a bad round of golf the next day and blame me for it. I had fulfilled this essential criterion of being an Indian girl. Now, I could start my new life.

As I went off with my husband, my father said, not joking at all, "She's your problem now." He immediately looked 20 years younger.

While that stress was relieved off my family, a new strange world was waiting for me: The world of being a married woman.

Being married comes with all the gleeful visions of finally being able to do those crazy things that were prohibited and frowned upon, while living under your family's watchful eye — prance around in shorts, stay out past midnight, drink wine for dinner. Your husband has to deal with you now!

But, before you're truly permitted to exploit your marital status with rebellious zeal, Indian culture has one last laugh at your freedom by shackling you to bridal bangles during the beginning of your newlywed life.

These bangles, or *choora*, are primarily worn by Hindu and Sikh brides as a custom which originated in Punjab. Being of Punjabi origin, I got to partake in this experience during my own *shaadi* (wedding).

Normally, consisting of a set of red and white bangles, the choora is gifted to the bride by her maternal uncle and aunt on her wedding morning. A full set can go all the way up to the elbow but I whittled it down to 31 bangles, covering about halfway up my wrist. I couldn't imagine being cuffed like the women who came before me such as my grandmother who didn't have a choice or say in the matter.

Traditionally, married women are supposed to keep the bangles on at all times until she reaches her first wedding anniversary. She should also dress like a bride for some time while she is a newlywed. The exception is only if the bride gets pregnant before the one-year mark, because who wants to be chained to bangles and a baby.

Besides signifying your marital status, wearing the bangles is meant to represent fertility and success. It is also worn for the well-being of your husband, although I'm not quite sure how that works when you accidentally smack him in your sleep while tossing and turning, or just smack him in general because you're irritated being stuck wearing constricting bangles and he's not.

Modern brides also have the option of wearing *choora* for a minimum of 40 days after her wedding for the sake of convenience and as a sort of "honeymoon" from doing anything related to housework or heavy lifting for over a month.

In other instances, some families say a bride should wear her choora until another relative gets married, which is what I chose to follow. I surprised myself for how dedicated I was to this custom as I never took my bangles off even when I went to the gym. I guess I saw it as an added weight for my workout.

People were shocked at my traditionalism as I had often projected myself to be the opposite — I married a non-Indian after all.

But that's the thing about traditions — they may not be practical for everyday living but there is a timeless beauty in a shared ritual. That's what drew me to keeping on my choora.

When my first cousin got married seven months later, my bangles were removed in some sort of ritual that involved money and *mithai* (Indian sweets), just like all Hindu ceremonies. I immediately booked a waxing appointment to take care of the hair that had been growing on my forearm under the accessories. But I experienced another strange sensation — I felt bare. The attention I had received as a new bride vanished. The choora had instantly accessorized all my outfits. I could wear a sweatshirt and still look dressed up with the bangles peeking out from the sleeves.

Suddenly, I had all this freedom and I didn't know what to do with it. I was no longer a newlywed to be admired. Now, I was just another married girl nagging her husband. Where were my parents telling me how to act? Where was my mom asking me what I wanted to eat for dinner? How was I supposed to behave now?

Luckily, the benevolent aunties of society were quick to put me in my place whenever I was seen in public not looking like a wedded woman.

"Beti, you're not wearing any earrings? Nothing on your wrists? Here, take my bangle and wear it, you can't leave your arm bare like that!"

After I got married, these comments came from every angle. I quickly learned that wedded Indian women should always have something on her ears and wrists, even after we take our choora off, as an auspicious sign that no other men should try to pick us up. This rule was still pushed on me despite marrying someone of a different culture, as I was meant to represent our Indian traditions and keep them alive, maybe even more excessively so that I wouldn't lose myself to a Swiss-Chinese world.

The amount of jewelry an Indian bride wears, especially gold, is a sign of her family's esteem. It makes the society and her husband's family see her worth.

Many factors of a married woman's appearance are also linked to traditions and culture. While it may vary by region or religion, Hindu women are known to wear *sindoor* (a red powder that is streaked in the middle parting of their hair). Besides symbolizing married status, it has its roots in Hindu spirituality for awakening the chakra of the "third eye". There are a number of beautiful meanings and values behind a lot of these traditions, but they are easily lost and desecrated among each generation. I only wore the sindoor on my wedding day as a nod to tradition but couldn't imagine adding it to my already hectic daily morning routine.

Losing out to the diamond engagement ring for daily wear is the *mangalsutra*. It is an auspicious thread that a groom ties around his bride's neck on the day of their wedding. It symbolically represents the uniting of two souls. Another reason the wife wears it is to ensure a long life and good health of her husband. Contrary to the traditional belief that a married woman should never keep it away from her neck, I took mine off the day after my wedding. Mr. Swiss-Chinese never forced me to wear it for his protection. In fact, he asked me what he was supposed to do to ensure my long life and good health, but I told him I would need to handle that myself.

On a less ceremonial level, married women face scrutiny for dressing appropriately and acting demurely as to not embarrass their new family-in-law. We're still required to keep ourselves modestly covered and bend ourselves to fit in with our new life, and this was no different in a non-Indian family.

The rules are adjusted depending on the house you are married into. If you have landed into a joint family who lives under one roof — in-laws, grandparents, aunts, uncles, cousins — you can forget about walking around bra-less, or even having your bra straps exposed, because that's one of the many sights considered inappropriate. I unwittingly took these rules with me as precaution around my family-in-law to show I was raised "right". After all, maybe I never stopped to consider the alternative perspective: that it was challenging for them to have an Indian daughter-in-law as well. They accommodated cooking for me in a separate pan when they ate beef, they graciously attended numerous days of wedding functions and accepted that money and sweets had to be given when they met all my relatives.

One universal truth about marriage that I learned was all your choices will continue to be analyzed no matter what family you land into. Now you have inherited more people who will check to make sure you are doing everything for your husband's comfort and to blend in with their ways.

If you are lucky enough to have your own private space, you will still be required to change out of your pajamas when the in-laws pop in for a surprise visit, again to ensure that you are taking good care of their little *raja.*

Single or married, Indian or non-Indian, it sure is hard to be a woman.

CHAPTER 13

Very Superstitious

As much as I tried to deny and suppress the conservative influence of my family, certain cultural elements managed to creep into my psyche and illogically affect my own thinking against my better judgement.

This became apparent to me while I was at the airport with my husband, about to board the plane for our honeymoon to Cairo, Egypt. I should have been romanticizing about all the fun we would have now that we were legally wedded and weren't traveling in sin, according to my parents' eyes. Finally, I would be able to openly post social media photos of my husband and me posing in front of the pyramids and riding on camels, without adjusting my privacy settings each time. But the only thing I could think about was… sugar.

We had forgotten to have a pinch of sugar before leaving home!

Before embarking on any road or plane trip, my mom had always made us eat a few grains of sugar as we were about to leave the house. Quite literally it was supposed to ensure a sweet and safe journey.

The superstition had been whittled down from a belief in India about eating a concoction of curd and sugar before important events like exams, business deals or job interviews to offer good luck.

My brothers and I had always rolled our eyes at this practice, especially with me complaining about how I didn't want to eat raw sugar for the sake of my figure (never mind the packs of biscuits I copiously consumed).

After eating the sugar, we weren't allowed to go back into the house, which made it very difficult if we had forgotten something. We moaned and groaned but took in the sweetness anyway to appease my mom.

Now, I was free from this tradition and able to make my own choices, but here I was at the airport scrambling to find a sugar packet from a coffee shop. I frantically made my husband have some of the sweetened crystals before we got on the plane, while he was quite bemused by the silent realization that I was slowly becoming my mother.

That's the thing no one tells you about growing up; we spend so much time battling our parents that we never listen to or do what they say. Then one day, we find ourselves taking part in the very things that we fought against when it comes to the protection of our own families.

Of course, there are other instances where you do have to draw the line.

Superstitions abound in Indian culture. The myths can vary based on what region you are from and what your family background dictates, but mostly it intersects with religion and astrology. This makes it a touchy subject.

Growing up, I was blitzed with beliefs about the most trivial things: what day I could wash my hair, the most auspicious time to cut my locks or nails, when it was a good time to make donations to charity, certain foods that were forbidden on specific days… it was never-ending. Plus, the answers were always different depending on who you asked.

Luckily, I didn't absorb the exact days in question. I would never be able to maintain a carefree life if I was constricted and fearful of such superstitions.

There were times I would be laying on the couch watching TV and minding my own business, when suddenly my mom would hover above me circling a lime three times around my head, basing it on a belief that it could remove any ill energy cast on a person.

You could not get my mom to respond to anything when she would be watching religious figures on Indian channels in their bright saffron robes and prayer beads around their neck. Her children asking for snacks or fighting in the background were ignored. She took in every word they said as if it was the only voice that existed.

To say she is religious is an understatement; it's like saying Gandhi was just some skinny, bald, bespectacled Indian dude. She wakes up at 5 a.m. every morning and the first thing she does is clean the *mandir* (a Hindu or Jain temple) at home, placing fresh orange and yellow marigolds in front of each deity's figure. She is a strict vegetarian, prays daily, goes to the temple every Monday and looks for an opportunity to go again whenever there is a religious event. She arranges all the pujas for occasions including birthdays, anniversaries, Diwali, children's births, whenever she feels the need to summon and thank the Gods. She fasts regularly, probably more times in a week than she eats — moon fast, Monday fast, Lord Shiva fast, Lord Ganesha fast and so on. No one can slow her down.

My mom's religious tendencies were ingrained from her childhood, an example of a first-generation Thai who was able to honor and abide by her Indian roots. She accompanied her grandmother to the temple every day, and found solace in the rituals and prayers involved. They would sit in a tuk-tuk at 5 a.m. ready to get their blessings for the day. Her family had certain pundits and gurus they followed religiously and would accommodate them at their home whenever they came from India, feeding and hosting them royally. Being exposed to such customs from a young age solidified her interest in religion, but surprisingly it never passed on to us with such intensity. Perhaps, since my mom prayed so much for her family and children, her words kept us eternally protected.

While we all tried to leave a puja to check our phones or find something to eat, my mom would sit diligently without moving for an entire hour, reciting the same holy Sanskrit chants and prayers along with the pundit.

The only time I have ever had multiple missed calls from my mother — besides to ask if I would be home for dinner — was when there was some astronomical event going on.

"There's an eclipse tomorrow. Don't eat or cook any food between 10 a.m. and 2 p.m.," she advised, ignoring the fact that I might feel hunger regardless of what the planets decide to do.

"I'm just letting you know what I have learned. Follow it if you want," she would remark in the same guilt-inducing tone parents use when they say they're "disappointed" in you. She never offered any explanation, it just had to be done. I then had to search for the answers online myself so I could at least have an understanding of why my mom felt the need to be constantly guided by forces bigger than ourselves.

I learned she was referring to an Ayurvedic belief that bacteria are more active when there is no sun (never mind modern hygiene practices), thus we should refrain from handling food. An eclipse is even worse if you're pregnant, because your Indian mother will surely bombard you with age-old knowledge, adding to the annoyance you already feel from your shifting hormones.

So, of course, there was a solar eclipse during my first pregnancy. My mom made sure I didn't leave the house. "Don't even look outside because it could cause harm to your baby," she frantically warned me, as if I didn't have enough to worry about. A bag full of basil leaves was also mysteriously dropped off at my door with no note or explanation. I called my mom, who confirmed she was the sender and told me to immediately put them under the four corners of my bed so that the eclipse would not affect my unborn child.

"But mom, won't it attract ants or bugs or something? I don't want to sleep with it there."

"Just put it there, why do you have to question everything I say? Listen sometimes, I'm trying to help you, you make everything so difficult. I don't hear anyone else asking such nonsense all the time. I said put the basil under your bed, I'm not telling you to stand on your head."

After she hung up abruptly without saying goodbye, agitated and annoyed, as evidenced by her usual run-on rants, I acquiesced and did as she said, carrying on with my day (in fact, the basil might still be under my bed, I'm not sure if I ever took it out). Through my own Googling, I learned that basil is meant to have anti-radiation properties, so it is believed it can neutralize any negative impacts from an eclipse.

Well, mom, why didn't you just say that?

Color also plays a big role for us Indians. Take for example red; (almost) every bride wears the color; traditional bindis/ *tikka* reflect the pigment, and it's used excessively in religious and auspicious events.

My family is not a fan of black or white, owing to its morbid symbolism at joyous events. Indians believe black is unholy and negative, while white is traditionally the color worn at funerals. Never mind that fashion experts say it can make you look slimmer or fresher. Anytime I wear these two hues, I get the sort of drained, peeved look from my parents that say: "You know how much we dislike it when you wear black or white, why do you keep doing it and aggravating us when you could just have a happier existence and make our lives better by wearing pink, red, yellow or any other color!"

Indian parents have a knack for saying a lot with just a glance.

These color superstitions affected my ability to dress freely without judgment. However, I had to remind whoever would listen that I'm sure somewhere in the world, there is probably a really terrible person who has committed a truly heinous crime or begotten some misfortune while wearing red.

The superstitions really came to life when I birthed new life (thankfully a healthy one, perhaps courtesy of the basil). When I had my first baby, everyone in my Indian community had many suggestions on how to protect my child.

Aunties were appalled I didn't draw a line of black kohl behind my son's ear or tie a holy thread on his wrist to ward off the evil eye when I took him out in public.

My grandmother, forever terrified that even complimenting my baby would cause *nazar* (attract the evil eye), burned red chilies on an open flame to get rid of any negative energy that may have afflicted him. She, however, disregarded the fact that the smell of burnt spice in the house would cause other afflictions for us.

It is perhaps growing up with this level of extremism that led me to take a more restrained approach towards religion and superstition.

Thankfully, it has all seemed to turn out fine.

Touch wood.

CHAPTER 14

Sari Not Sari

ONE common feature of traditional Indian womenswear is exposed bellies. Whether through a lehenga or sari, all kinds of midriffs are on display — some tummies are big, some are small, some are filled with curry and some with dal.

There are generally no objections or labels of indecency when bare stomachs come out to play in Indian attire. I would prance around many of my wedding functions showing my closed-up belly button piercing and "tramp stamp" in front of hundreds of guests. Attendees would don backless blouses, plunging necklines and sheer fabrics. It almost seemed like a fashion show of Indian clothing miles away from India, in a community that could hold on to its culture by keeping updated on the latest clothes.

In my years of going to events that required Indian clothing, I've never been reprimanded for wearing what is essentially a glorified bra with my lehenga or sari. Stomach rolls, back fat, love handles — all of these are fair game when revealed in Indian clothing.

But why is it that the same look, worn in the form of Western attire, elicits disapproving reactions?

When the ratio of skin to stretch marks were skewed in my favor, my closet had a sizable number of crop tops. But the moment even a bit of my bloated tummy was on display, it was deemed inappropriate (and possibly offensive to show a stomach that's allergic to sit-ups). My mom would remind me again that I was "basically naked" and no one would marry me if I dressed up like that.

My brother enjoyed chiming in, making some offhand joke about how I was so poor that I didn't have enough money to buy a whole shirt.

Funny fact, I was wearing a crop top and shorts — double taboo! — the night I met the man who would become my husband.

Why is there this contradiction between revealing the same body part in different cultural contexts?

Perhaps it's because of the context of the clothes itself. Ancient Indian tradition suggests that the navel of the Supreme Being (Vishnu) is revered as the source of life and creativity. Thus, midriffs were left bare in clothing as a symbol of honor and worship, as well as to possibly attract good energy. You don't want to cover up the source of existence after all!

It appears this same symbolism isn't applied to non-Indian wear, where showing the midriff perhaps only means exhibiting whether you have an innie or outie, or flaunting the fact that you can eat 50 *gulab jamuns* (an Indian sweet dish) a day without getting fat.

This Western format of dressing can feel foreign to people who have only ever seen the same body parts displayed in Indian clothing. To them, a crop top draped with a sari is elegant, but a crop top paired with booty shorts is unfamiliar.

What would people say if they also knew that way back in the day, some women draped sari fabric over their body with no shirt on at all? The existence of the sari has been traced back to the Indus Valley Civilization where people wrapped themselves with a cotton cloth to suit the hot climate.

Notions of decorum as practiced today were imported by the British and other cultures that came into contact with India. Rulers of the British Raj introduced blouses to be worn under saris as part of high fashion based on their perceptions of propriety, and this spread as the "traditional" benchmark of modesty. This might help explain why the English terms "blouse" and "petticoat" are used to describe elements of Indian clothing. What we accept as principles of Indian modesty may very well turn out not to be Indian at all.

Bare boobs do not make a bare belly seem so scandalous now, right?

Indian attire isn't generally designed to display the lower limbs. It can be quite a curious sight when a "good girl" willingly chooses to show her ingrown hairs on her legs, which her waxing lady couldn't remove.

Branded as "underwear" in my house, shorts are the one item that evoked equal disgust across generations from my mother to my grandmother. Wearing them in front of my relatives was akin to being caught French kissing a non-Indian boy in broad daylight. Anything above the knee was considered to be bad form.

The only time I could freely wear shorts was if I took a beach trip with my friends without my family present. Those trips were fashionably liberating because I didn't have to think about all the ways to cover up or stress about any outfits being objectionable. I could tap into the dark depths of my wardrobe which housed restricted items like shorts, spaghetti straps, miniskirts, tube tops and bikinis.

I didn't choose these clothes because I was purposely trying to expose myself. I felt confident wearing them. The revealing nature didn't carry a stigma to me.

In our imperfect world, women are still victimized for how they dress. Clothes can unfairly attract the wrong kind of attention, therefore, my family tried hard to make sure I didn't put myself in dangerous situations by dressing provocatively.

Besides being a way to judge your character, an Indian family can also see clothes as a way of displaying prestige. Nothing has conjured more controversy and jests than ripped jeans, mocked as "pants for homeless people". This is a trend that almost every elderly and righteous Indian I've ever met couldn't accept.

"Did we not give you everything?" my mom would wail. "The best schools, the best home, the best life. Why do you have to walk around in those torn pants?"

"Are you going to collect the trash in those clothes?" my dad would snicker.

I always found these reactions a bit exaggerated. After all, ripped jeans are an article of clothing that is deliberately dysfunctional — they don't really serve any practical purpose to the wearer except maybe to air out their thighs or knees on a hot day.

They have their historical associations with rocker and grunge movements which have entered into the fashion mainstream and is expected to make a seasonal reemergence. Its unfavorable reputation means it still remains on the inappropriate list for such locations as country clubs, workplaces, schools, at the wedding altar, on the golf course and of course in the eyes of your Indian family.

However, ripped jeans can be viewed as a styling challenge. It is the wearer's responsibility to not go full-on with the "bum look", but rather prove that it can be worn in a sophisticated and dressed up way. Hole-y denim works wonderfully to contrast the formality of a tailored blazer; it can minimize the stuffiness of a dress shirt; accessorize it with some lace-up heels and you are ready for a night out, even though you should be staying home.

No one listened or sympathized anyway, as they were too busy telling me how Auntie Twinkle's daughter never dressed like that and how they were so unlucky to get a daughter who wasted time wearing pants that had holes.

There is no rulebook floating around somewhere documenting notions of decency. A lot of these ideas about safety or appropriateness linked to our clothes have been constructed over time as a knee-jerk reaction to terrible crimes committed against women.

When you're part of a culture that is still finding the balance between antiquated traditions and modern liberties, certain items of clothing and lifestyle choices evoke controversy. Indian women all over the world — as well as those from similar societies — are having to toe the line between honoring the wishes of their family/community and embracing their own individuality.

When it was time to buy a dress for my eighth-grade middle school dance, one of my many generous aunts stepped into the picture. It would be the first dance I ever attended and my aunt wanted to do something nice. She took me dress shopping.

I was already feeling bad about the whole thing because my friends were all getting ready together but my mom wouldn't let me join in: "You don't have your own house? You have to go get dressed in other people's rooms?" she quipped, in her signature backwards question form that didn't leave room for an answer. In the same way, she was totally against sleepovers too: "You don't have your own bed to sleep in? You have to go lie down on someone else's floor? You want people to think we are poor?"

As I wandered through the selection of clothes at the department store, I longingly gazed at beautiful velvet dresses with spaghetti straps, halter necks and criss-crosses on the back. I didn't dare ask if I could buy them, let alone try them on.

It didn't matter anyway. My aunt's face lit up — "I found the best one!" She held up a hanger featuring a pastel knee-length shift dress. It was color-blocked with a pale-yellow shade on the top half and pink on the bottom starting from the hip. It wasn't particularly nice or trendy but I was amazed she picked something sleeveless.

"And here's the matching jacket!"

Groan.

I didn't know how to say "no" without sounding ungrateful, so that was the dress I ended up getting. I wore it to the dance feeling extra frumpy next to my friends who had all done trendy things like crimping their hair and lathering glitter lotion all over their arms and legs for an extra shimmer.

It was sweet that my aunt was protective of me and wanted to keep me safe… as a girl. But I felt powerless then and even sometimes now.

CHAPTER 15

Becoming a Desi Girl

As an Indian living outside of India, my knowledge and exposure to the ethnic clothing of my motherland was embarrassingly limited. Clothes are one of the first ways someone can identity where you are from and what you represent. Western brands and styles of clothing worked its way into my brain via commercial stores, magazines, TV/movies, celebrities and more recently, social media influencers. If your foreign house didn't have a subscription to Zee TV or Star World India, you would rarely see the daily Indian way of dressing as portrayed by the archetypal characters in serials. Through my grandmother's shows, I had come to welcome the demure daughter covered up in a plain salwar or the conniving mother-in-law in her showy sari and glittering yellow gold jewels, into my living room every afternoon.

Even when I visited India, I felt like nothing more than an awestruck tourist. The immigration officer at Indira Gandhi International Airport in New Delhi did not appreciate the fact that I couldn't understand what he was saying when I handed over my Thai passport: "You don't speak Hindi? But you look Indian, your name is Indian, your family is Indian."

(Funnily enough, I received the opposite judgment living in Thailand: "You can speak Thai? But you look Indian, your name is Indian, your family is Indian.")

On the way to our hotel, my brothers and I would have the same astonished reaction to the chaotic streets of India, no matter how many times we had seen it before. The honking pandemonium on the roads, the heroic death-defying jaywalking of locals and the number of stray cows roaming freely never failed to culture-shock us. When I finally reached the peace of the hotel room and started unpacking my suitcase, I recalled the horrified response my parents had when they saw its contents back in Bangkok.

Each piece of clothing was sprawled out on my bedroom floor and carefully vetted by my mom and/or dad before they were approved for travel to India. Only full-length pants, and blouses with long sleeves were allowed, nothing low cut, skimpy or sheer. There was no room for anything that could remotely give off a whiff of sexiness or indication that a woman existed underneath.

I thought I was quite shrewd when skinny jeans became popular — now I could argue that I was still covered up from hip to ankle but sexily show off my gams. One look at the frame-fitting silhouette and my mom shot back with her signature ridicule: "Why do you even bother wearing pants?

Just take them off then, and walk around naked. Who are you trying to fool?"

For a long time, I didn't understand why I had to be *even more* covered up in India. My parents brushed it off in one simple motto: "Don't draw attention to yourself." Obviously, that was not well-received by a young girl swayed by style magazines, who believed she was a fashionista and the world was her unlimited runway. My vision — wearing leather shorts with an off-shoulder bohemian blouse, paired with a scarf I would buy at a local market in Delhi, while taking the perfect OOTD picture posing next to a chai wala stand — was ripped away from me.

I only comprehended why females needed to be cloaked and concealed as I got older. When I went back to India as a teenager, I could sense the male gaze on me almost everywhere I went. It was nothing like I had experienced in Bangkok. The grandparents who came before us had tried to replicate India in our little Bangkok community by bringing over the same language, food and customs. They had passed on these traits to their children as their way of holding on to being Indian. But maybe all the rules didn't apply anymore because life in India was not the same as Bangkok.

The stares were piercing, its intention seemed different, it was unwanted. Before I even saw men looking at me, I could already feel it. The funny thing was that what I wore didn't change how or if men looked at me. Even if I was covered up, they still stared. I was extremely self-conscious. I pulled the cardigan a little tighter around my chest and shoulders.

Merely being a woman warranted the staring, the curiosity and the leering. It was the burden we had to shoulder as women in a male-dominated and conservative society where women are still viewed as objects. This belief seeps into our attire and our traditions.

My parents' simple motto resonated in my head: "Don't draw attention to yourself."

Oh, that's what they meant.

My parents would have much preferred if I wore a nice long cotton kurta with thick leggings, which they viewed as the responsible way of dressing for an Indian girl. That didn't translate as an ideal choice beyond India for me and I had no desire to look like I was fresh off the rickshaw.

Jeans and tank tops (with a sweater or shawl when in the presence of conservative eyes) was the mode of dressing I chose, largely because that's what I was most exposed to. As a young girl, I only owned two salwar kameez with an unsightly net overlay that seemed to snag and tear at every turn. These were purchased for me in India by family friends because my parents were tired of seeing me wear inappropriate dresses to Indian-centric functions.

With no say in the style or size, I looked terrible whenever I reluctantly wore any of those outfits. I looked out of touch with my Indian-ness in the ill-fitting outfits and as a matter of fact, I was. Therefore, I spent my time perfecting and focusing on Western styles of dressing.

My early experiences of wearing Indian clothing started with salwar kameez. The pants were always too baggy while the shirt too oversized Going to the bathroom was like getting ready for a marathon. How do you sit down without dipping your *chunni* in the toilet? Then you have to simultaneously untie and re-tie the drawstring on the pants so it doesn't fall down.

Before ready-made saris and salwars, I couldn't get behind the concept of the unstitched salwar kameez. It was so off-putting that you couldn't buy off the rack, especially for someone who loves clothes and the thrill of carrying a shopping bag home. Not to mention the awkwardness of getting measured by a tailor who usually got something wrong with the finished piece, thus resulting in further delays of getting the suit in time.

But what really baffled me was the constant struggle with the safety pin to get the chunni sitting perfectly on the shoulder. I didn't know how to do it myself, and I could never find anyone who was able to clip the fabric on my shoulder without the safety pin tackily showing. Even then I didn't know how to pleat the dupatta correctly so I looked especially dowdy.

Saris were particularly complicated. It's an art to be able to tie the whole thing so it stays on, plus the added step of stitching a blouse and petticoat to match it. Sari-tying is an actual business in Bangkok — ladies come to your house to help you drape your sari before an event. It is a niche and necessary need for a society that attempts to stay Indian. I was absolutely not interested in going through all these steps to get ready; a regular dress was much less complicated.

As Bollywood celebrities gained more presence in the world stage and started bringing their glittering looks to red carpet events, the beauty and intricacies of Indian fashion started being recognized by those of us who were previously clueless, like myself sitting in my Bangkok bubble. As I gained more exposure to Indian styles of dressing, I started appreciating the beauty of the designs — the detailed embroidery, the mirror work, the graphic prints. I didn't need a plane ticket to India to see what was cool, but just an internet connection. I clicked through various portals showcasing Indian outfits and soaked up the beauty.

Suddenly, I didn't only want to rock Western fashion, but also feel stunning in Indian clothes, in all their complicated layers and glory.

This complication is what makes it beautiful. It's rare to find two Indian women who show up to a party wearing an identical outfit. Each outfit isn't mass-produced and it's commonplace to have every item custom-fit to your specific figure, even if it takes the tailor a few tries to get it right.

Then, you add the jewelry; Indian jewelry doesn't come to a party to sit silently in the back. The pieces are big and dazzling, they are here to be seen in all their yellow gold and bejeweled glory.

One summer on one of my annual trips to India with my family, I decided to get my nose pierced. While in India I started seeing women everywhere, even little girls, with their nose pierced. It looked so beautiful, so distinctly "Indian". I asked my parents if I could do it because we as kids always need to ask for permission no matter how old we are and surprisingly they agreed. To them it was also something in line with my culture.

I remember how horrified they had been when they found out I had secretly pierced my belly button and tongue in high school and then eyebrow in college. That was a fun greeting at the airport when I came off the flight and surprised them with the latest addition to my face.

Previously, Indian clothing had always been sold to me as a way to cover up, to show humility — "drape the dupatta over your chest, use it to hide your open back, put it over your head."

Now, it could be showcased for its beauty, extraordinary craftsmanship and hints of liberation.

It can make even a non-Indian girl feel a little more Indian.

We wear miniskirts because we love every part of our body.
We wear pants because we feel cold, not because an
auntie told us to cover up.
We challenge what society dictates to find our freedom.
We should all dress our body and mind without fear.

Acknowledgements

ONE Saturday morning, I attended a manifestation workshop in Bangkok. I didn't know what exactly I hoped to get out of this — we all have so many desires, so many things we wish for, sometimes in conflict with reality. My higher self was lost somewhere in the monotony of routine. In a rush to get back home to my scheduled programming, I put exactly one thing on the vision board we had to create during the workshop: an image of a book cover with my title on it.

On Tuesday evening, I received a WhatsApp message from Nu Voice Press. They had come across my book proposal — the one for the manuscript I had completed in 2022 but hadn't been picked up by any other publishing houses. They were interested in collaborating to make my book a reality. To the Nu Voice team — thank you for your endless patience, trust and belief in my book. Whether I unknowingly manifested it or the literary stars were working in my favor, you have helped me reawaken my dreams.

In no particular order, I would also like to extend my gratitude to Jagdish Gill, my fellow confused Indian touchstone, for always being excited about my "sneak peeks" and her unwavering championing of all my work.

To Mim Koletschka for reading the first draft when it was just a sloppy Microsoft Word document pretending to be a "book", helping me find the meaning of my sentences and pushing me to reveal more.

To Tara Rattanaphas and Diane Piroon, although each of you is in a category of your own, I put you together here because you never give up on your optimism and support for me even when I am lost.

To Veshali Sehgal, who roots for me, always.

I started writing as a way to make sense of the senseless. I didn't mean to grow up and become a writer — but it was the only profession I could think of where I could carve out a path that was truly my own.

To all those still finding the words — may you always have the courage to speak and live your fearless truth.

And always, thank you to my parents, who have lived this entire journey with me.

About the Author

Sumati Huber is an editor and columnist residing in Bangkok, Thailand. Growing up in a multicultural environment, humor and observation became her tools to navigate through the complexities of her Indian heritage amidst foreign cultural influences.

After earning a degree in English and Psychology from Emory University, she returned to Bangkok and joined *Guru*, a prestigious lifestyle magazine and weekly supplement of the *Bangkok Post*. She quickly rose to become the magazine's youngest editor, writing a popular weekly column that satirized local politics, current events and quirks of Thai society. It also garnered recognition from esteemed publications like *The New York Times*.

Currently, Sumati is a freelance columnist for *Masala*, a local Bangkok magazine. Her monthly column "Nama-Slay" enjoys a wide readership and continues to entertain and resonate with readers in the Thai-Indian community.